A YEAR OF RAIN

Jay Ishino

A Year of Rain

Paperback edition ISBN: 978-1-962420-05-1

E-book edition ISBN: 978-1-7370194-0-4

Library of Congress Control Number Available Upon Request.

This is a work of fiction. Names, characters, places, and incidents are either the product of the author's imagination or are used fictitiously. Any resemblance to actual persons, living or dead, events, or locales is entirely coincidental.

First edition: October 2021

Second Edition: August 2023

For more information contact jay@jayishino.com

Cover design by Wynter Designs.

Published by Sibyl Press, LLC

Chandler, Arizona

A YEAR OF RAIN

Jay Ishino

A Year of Rain

Paperback edition ISBN: 978-1-962420-05-1

E-book edition ISBN: 978-1-7370194-0-4

Library of Congress Control Number Available Upon
Request.

First edition: October 2021

Second Edition: August 2023

For more information contact jay@jayishino.com

Cover design by Wynter Designs.

Published by Sibyl Press, LLC

Chandler, Arizona

For A

My muse. For answering every single question I asked of you tirelessly, for telling me about your life, for supporting me during the beginning, the middle, and all the way to the end of this story, and most importantly for being my friend.

CONTENT WARNING

This book features scenes containing blood and gore, rope restraint, alcoholism, & miscarriage.

Author's Note

By and large, this book is a work of fiction. However, if you look carefully, you might find some recipes nestled in the chapters which could help you survive a post-apocalyptic world if ever you find yourself stuck in one. When cooking, as opposed to baking, precise measurements aren't necessary. Just make sure it tastes good to you. Remember to always double the amount of garlic any recipe calls for (trust me on this one), and don't forget the seasoning. One final thing: while I do not condone eating expired foods, sometimes one has to do what one needs to do in order to survive, especially in post-apocalyptic times. Good luck and happy eating!

PROLOGUE

RAIN DIDN'T LOVE DAN. Not anymore. Fine. He didn't love her anymore either, but he'd always been a good man, and he'd promised to protect her.

Earlier that week a scout had showed up at Rain's encampment, a lodge up in the mountains, with a message. She recognized Dan's handwriting and unmistakable signature almost at once. Fairly buzzed already, she stared hard at this short, heavily-armed man while she opened the note, scoffing loudly while silently reading the contents.

It had been an offer of protection and information on where and when to meet him. Everyone had heard about the wolf attack last full moon in the dense forest that surrounded the lodge. Three of Rain's people had been taken down by two wolves. Two had been killed and the third left for dead.

The fool dragged himself back to the lodge, dried blood caking his arms, highlighting the bites where he'd tried to fight off the creature. He said that after he passed out, the wolves must have assumed him dead and left him there.

Because he'd been bitten, he was already dead, at least to them. He would become a monster by the next full moon. As he stood in front of the lodge, tears streaking down his cheeks, he pleaded for his life. Without hesitation, Rain's friend, Seoyun, put a silver-tipped arrow through his skull.

After that, Seoyun sent her scouts to nearby survivor encampments, which had become few and far between in the past year. During food runs they'd found the sparse population of human survivors easy to keep track of. Word of the attack must have eventually reached Dan.

Rain folded the letter, pinching the creases hard and put it in one of the pockets of her gray cargo pants. Then she got stupid drunk and passed out. In the morning, as a courtesy, she told Seoyun her plan.

"I'm going." Rain shoved a few shirts and a couple pairs of pants into a backpack. "To stay with Dan for a while."

"What?" Seoyun's voice oozed disbelief more than confusion.

"I said I'm going to stay with Dan."

"You don't even love him anymore," Seoyun said, as if they'd had this conversation about Rain's ex a million times.

"But we have history," Rain mumbled.

"If you leave, do not come back." Seoyun's words, coated with ice, sounded like a curse. "And you will be miserable."

"Maybe I deserve to be miserable." Rain said, louder than she'd wanted to.

Now, as she walked through the forest, bright sunshine beaming through the trees, Rain replayed this conversation in her head many times.

After the attack, Rain had felt more and more unsafe, and Dan's letter boasted a large camp of survivors. At the lodge with Seoyun, their numbers had continued to dwindle.

After walking for a while, she decided to rest and drink some water. Sitting on a log, Rain spotted a clump of grass that looked like it had been combed over. When she peeled back the grass, she uncovered a quail's nest. She couldn't see any mother in sight, so she took a small pouch out of her backpack and draped it across her body. She plucked four eggs from the nest and tucked them into the pouch.

Rain smiled with the knowledge that she'd at least have some offering to repay Dan's generosity. When she turned to continue on her way, she stepped in a pile of leaves concealing a divot in the ground, and her foot got stuck in a tree root buried there. She moved to extract it but instead twisted it in an unnatural, painful way and went down.

She didn't know how long she laid there cursing and crying, but when she finally pulled herself up, the sun had traveled a considerable distance in the sky. Dusk. Having no desire to be traipsing through the forest at night, she willed herself to get up.

It soon became impossible to hobble across the unsteady ground of the forest floor, and Rain fell more times than she ever would have admitted to anyone.

More than once she crashed into a tree, where low, drooping branches scraped her arms. Some collisions occurred with such force the branches sliced her arms until they bled. Her pouch, full of tiny smashed eggs, ended up on the forest floor.

Each time Rain got up, she worried that she might not be going the right direction, and darkness now blanketed the forest, making her path not only uncertain but more precarious. Exhaustion and pain seemed to be the only feelings she was capable of anymore.

When she left, she'd been sure that there wouldn't be a full moon tonight, but the next time she fell she could have sworn she heard a howl.

She buried her face in the underbrush and sobbed. A wolf out there somewhere would come for her, so she decided to let it. She could go no farther and shrugged out of her backpack. All the energy had drained from her body, and she closed her eyes, hoping the wolf would kill her fast enough for her not to suffer.

When Rain opened her eyes, it hadn't been to a wolf gnawing on her femur. Nighttime shadows still danced across the trees in the forest, and she dragged her body to the nearest trunk and propped herself against it.

She leaned her head back and looked up at a sliver of the half moon through the trees. Moving her eyes back down into the forest, another light caught her eye. She blinked several times to be sure she hadn't hallucinated the slight shimmering in the distance.

1 FRIED EGGS

RAIN HADN'T HALLUCINATED. It was a cabin all right. The faint light she'd seen before now emitted a bright glow from the windows. Daring to inch closer, she dragged her leg and gripped her arm where streaks of dried blood painted her skin.

Rain heard the soft strumming of a guitar. When she got close enough to see porch steps in front of her, she fell to her knees. The music inside stopped, the shuffling sounds of movement taking its place.

Then the door creaked open as if pushed by the wind. Orange light from a fire danced through the porch railing, connected to two support beams running to an extension of the roof. A dark figure moved in between the beams, backlit from the soft illumination inside.

The darkness shrouded the stranger's face.

Hair, which stirred a little in the breeze, barely brushed the slim figure's broad shoulders. It was definitely a man. While she couldn't make out any distinct features on his face, she recognized a shotgun when she was staring into the barrel of one.

"Stop moving," the stranger said.

Rain froze at the sound of his cool, powerful voice which barely stirred the air around her.

"Please," she said, trying to raise her injured arm.

"Were you bitten?"

Realization spread across her face. *She* was a threat to him, not the other way around. A bloodied woman pleading for help and limping toward his home. What else could she be?

"No, I wasn't. I promise."

The man did not lower the shotgun. "Why are you limping? And what happened to your arms?"

"I fell," she said. "I twisted my ankle and scratched up my arms on some branches."

"Only scratches? No bites?" He still did not lower his weapon.

"I swear."

"I'll have to inspect it myself." He finally lowered the shotgun. "Come on. Let's get you patched up."

Heaving a great sigh of relief, she moved closer to the bottom of the porch steps, dragging her leg as she went. The stranger met her there and helped her walk up the three steps. His touch was gentle rather than forceful—a stark contrast to her first impression of him. She exhaled in relief.

"Thank you." She puffed out heavy breaths as she climbed.

"You're welcome." His voice was soft and sincere and again, so different from before.

He led her inside and helped her sit down at a table near the kitchen. Surprised, she looked the place over. It wasn't very big, but the design coupled with its high ceiling made it look spacious.

A wide-columned stone fireplace, outfitted with metal racks for cooking, stood in the center of the great room, splitting it into two sections. One section of the room boasted a huge sofa with a low table in front of it. Behind it stood a wall made entirely of recessed shelves full of books. Cushy chairs surrounded the fireplace on the both sides. It seemed like every chair in this cabin, even the one she sank into now, had been placed here with nothing but comfort in mind.

As he inspected her injuries, she became aware he tried to find bites or saliva—any indication she had lied to him, even though she hadn't. She knew he had no reason to trust someone he didn't know, especially the way things were these days. She wouldn't trust a stranger, either.

Seemingly satisfied she'd been honest with him, he began to dab at her cuts with pieces of alcohol-dampened fabric. She hissed and winced softly, and he started talking to her, perhaps to distract her.

"I'm Henry," he said, with a slight enthusiasm.

"Oh . . . Rain. I mean my name's Rain," she said, used to the confusion that came with introducing herself.

His voice was even and calm, and though deep, it never came out loud or jarring. The tone lulled her as he talked about mundane things. He didn't pry into her history or ask her any personal questions. He spoke to her in a way that let her volunteer any information she wanted to tell him. Likewise, he offered little information about himself.

Rain decided she liked Henry, this gentle and kind man. More than that, she'd gotten herself beyond lost and could use a real friend right now.

When he finished bandaging her arm, she noticed he held it a little too long, but this didn't bother her. His touch wasn't aggressive or offensive. It seemed . . . natural.

"I have never met anyone with better skin," he said, grazing his fingers along her arm as he let go.

Rain felt her face warm, hoping he didn't notice. She didn't need to be swooning over a stranger, no matter how kind he'd been to her. If Henry had noticed her blushing, he didn't say anything about it.

"Okay," he said after a long pause. "Let's look at that ankle."

Sitting across from her still, he pulled her injured leg up on top of his thigh. She felt no pain when he did this. He moved like someone handling a rare antique vase worth a lot of money.

"I'm afraid I don't have ice," he said. "But I can bandage this, and you'll need to stay off it and keep it elevated for a while. For a couple of days at least. Do you trust me to take care of you while this heals?"

Rain nodded, because as crazy as it sounded, for some reason she did trust this man she'd just met. He took extra-special care as he wrapped her ankle, tightening the bandage but checking with her to make sure he hadn't cut off her circulation.

"So you're going to need to sleep here on the couch, to help keep your leg elevated. Is that okay?"

"It's more than okay," Rain said, as she had not expected even a modicum of this level of care. "Thank you . . . for taking care of me."

She felt a twinge of shame saying this, as her stubbornness had often prevented her from admitting she needed help. However, she didn't have much choice. She had no idea where she'd ended up after tumbling around in the forest. She knew that she could never make it to Dan's encampment if she didn't heal. Trusting this stranger would be her best chance of getting to safety.

Henry helped her walk to the sofa, offering his arm so she didn't put too much weight on her ankle. Once she nestled into the cushions, she noticed his bright blue eyes, which shone like sea glass, almost penetrating her. She felt as if he could see inside her, which was equal parts thrilling and unsettling.

However, he simply asked her if she was hungry. "I've got some dried meats—"

"Oh," she cut him off. "I . . . um . . . I don't eat meat."

"That's okay. I can open a can of beans."

Because he didn't mention that in this world not eating meat was ridiculous, like so many others had before, a smile spread across Rain's lips. When she glanced from her ankle to his face, she noticed the corners of his mouth had also pulled up into a slight smile.

Her eyes grew heavy as she listened to Henry making soft clunking sounds in the kitchen. A can thumped on the counter. Dishes rattled. The clatter of a spoon sounded on a plate.

When Rain opened her eyes, she had no idea how much time had passed, but she knew she'd fallen asleep. Henry looked comfortable, curled up into a chair opposite the couch. When he saw her open her eyes, he peered over the book in his hands and then folded it upside down onto his knee.

"Good morning." His eyes bore into her as if he wanted to say something more than the greeting he'd just uttered.

"Is it?" Rain dug her knuckles into her eyes. "How long have I been asleep?"

"You slept through the night. Do you have to use the bathroom?"

He'd read her mind there, and her head bobbed with a nod laced with relief.

"There's no toilet in here," Henry said. "But there's an outhouse in the back. I'll help you to it."

Henry rose, extending his arm for Rain to grab onto. She gripped it and pulled herself up with a little wince after putting weight on her injury. He walked her to the back of the house, opening a door to a stone path leading to a small wooden outhouse.

Upon entering it, she found that it wasn't some old western outhouse. The door clicked behind her and she gazed around, feeling surprised that an outhouse impressed her.

It had been designed and built with the same level of skill as what little she'd seen of the interior of the cabin, and like any modern bathroom, there was a roll of toilet paper in a holder secured to the side. Rain wondered how Henry had come by that but felt lucky she'd met such a resourceful man.

Once finished, she pushed open the door, fully prepared to hop back to the house. But she saw Henry leaning on a nearby tree far enough away to give her some privacy. When he saw her emerge, he rushed to her side, and she clamped onto him, grateful he'd been serious about taking care of her.

Back on the comfortable couch, Rain felt far too tired for someone who'd only gone to the bathroom. She squeezed her eyes together, but Henry's voice jolted them open again.

"Do you eat eggs?" He knelt on the floor next to the sofa, speaking close to her in a low voice.

"Eggs? Oh yes, why? Do you have eggs?"

"Yes," Henry said. "I used to have chickens for a while. They were killed last month, but there are still some eggs left over. I can fry you a couple for breakfast, and we can eat those beans from last night."

Right. She'd passed out before she could eat anything last night, and her stomach screamed with the realization she hadn't eaten in who knew how long.

"That'd be really nice. Thank you, H."

Henry raised an eyebrow. "H?"

"It's cute right? Or is it too much?" Rain asked, feeling her neck grow hot.

"H is nice. I like H." He smiled, walking into the kitchen.

He emerged from the kitchen, carrying a plate of two fried eggs and warm beans on the side. She thanked him, and he slid into the chair across from her, eating with her.

A thick silence hovered in the air between them, the only sound that of forks on plates.

2 Garden Variety Vegetables

OVER THE NEXT FEW DAYS, Rain hobbled around the cabin anytime she needed something. Henry told her not to do this, that he would get her anything she needed, and she should rest to heal. But Rain felt she might be imposing on him and was determined not to trouble him further.

She'd crashed on his sofa, and though maybe it wasn't true, Rain feared he hadn't had a choice in the matter. The more she thought about it, the more she reasoned that Henry certainly had a choice. He had resolved to take care of Rain while she healed. He had allowed her to stay in his cabin. He had decided not to blow her head off with a shotgun. All conscious decisions.

Still Henry turned out to be a wonderful caretaker, though this included little. Most of the time, Rain felt content to just eat and stay off her ankle as much as possible.

Because of his kindness, she grew affectionate, more than she would have been with someone whose whole history she didn't know. She touched him whenever she could. Tender, simple touches were the only way she could thank him for everything he'd done for her.

One day, after a particular stretch of boredom consisting of watching the wind blow from her spot on the sofa, she asked Henry if he could find some vegetable seeds when he was on his way out to scavenge for food and supplies.

"You've got a green thumb?" he asked.

"I can grow things," she said.

"I'll find you some seeds." His voice sounded full of determination.

To other people it might have seemed strange to plant a garden in a stranger's yard, but Rain wanted to do something for Henry that would last after she left to meet up with Dan. A gift for all time.

"Before you go—" She cut herself off, hesitant to ask him for one more thing.

"Anything," he said.

"Do you have any science fiction books up there?" She gestured to the bookcase wall behind her.

"I think so," he said, crossing to the shelves.

He dragged his hands along the spines until

he stopped on one, and when he handed it to her, the frayed cover, decorated with a faded fluorescent spaceship, curled at the edges.

Her forehead wrinkled. "Looks old and weird."

He shrugged. "I just pick up whatever I can find out there."

"I'll try to enjoy it while you're gone," she said, offering him a slight smile.

He bade her farewell with a promise to return with a bounty of seeds. After he left, she opened the book, which puffed out a musty smell in response. A cheesy space opera from the 1970s, it was as enjoyable as watching people flail on a reality television show once had been.

Not too long after opening the book, she pushed it onto the table in front of the sofa. Her eyes felt heavy, and for a moment she wondered if it was because of the silly story or simple exhaustion.

She awoke to the sounds of Henry placing things on the kitchen counter.

"Sorry to wake you," he said.

Embarrassment colored her face, and she ran her fingers across a line in her cheek from the pillow. "I think I passed out . . . again."

"You definitely passed out." He walked over to her and dropped to one knee beside the sofa, producing several packages of seeds: broccoli, cauliflower, zucchini, carrots, celery, tomatoes, radishes, herbs, and many kinds of leaf vegetables.

Taking them in her hands, eyes wide, she couldn't hide the joy in her voice even if she had tried. "This is amazing!"

"Yeah?"

"Definitely. Thank you so much, Henry!"

Still holding the seeds, she attempted to wrap her arms around him, having difficulty getting a good grip due to her position on the sofa. But she tried to embrace him nonetheless.

"When I'm more mobile, I'll plant these."

"No rush," he said, returning to the kitchen to finish unpacking. "I also found some seed potatoes."

"I've decided something," she said, beaming up at him. "I like you better than most people."

He glanced over at her, a tiny grin forming. "I like you better than most people, too."

"You should probably know something about me. It's hard for me to like people immediately. I tolerate a lot of people at first. There are some I like, but I love even fewer than that."

"Me too," he said. "I'm a loner, so I like a lot of people but don't really want to spend time with most."

Her face relaxed, relieving some of the tension she felt, but now a twinge of attraction for Henry bubbled through her, as she ran her fingers over the seed packages.

"I need to sleep," he said.

She almost hadn't noticed the darkness that had seeped in through every window.

"Night." She spit out the word with a smile.

"Goodnight," he said, disappearing into the bedroom.

A couple of days later, even though it still ached to walk once in a while, Rain decided she felt much better than she had when she first arrived. After much deliberation, she convinced Henry to help walk her out to the front yard. The weather screamed prime planting season, and she grew anxious when she thought about missing it.

In a spot far enough away from the shade of the large maple tree in front of the cabin, she tore through the soft earth with her fingernails, as she had no gardening tools. The rich smell of quality soil, begging for crops, wafted up into her nostrils. Henry assisted by carrying buckets of water from the well on the side of the cabin.

A tight frown spread across her face when next he appeared from around the side of the house, carrying a shovel instead of a bucket of water. Tilting his head to the side, he shrugged and then went to work digging the serious trenches she'd requested for the potatoes. Finally, she planted all the seeds in rows by type, making sure the vegetables were spaced out properly.

"The radishes will grow the fastest," she said.

Eyes like a child full of endless curiosity,

Henry watched her work. He told her he had never thought of planting a garden here himself as he didn't possess the particular know-how but that he was happy Rain had decided to do this. He said he couldn't remember the last time he ate fresh vegetables and looked forward to doing so once again.

In all honesty, she didn't think she'd be around to see the lush crops. She already felt she'd overstayed her welcome by recovering here, and because Dan was expecting her, he'd soon have people looking for her.

Also, she didn't feel like she had the right to ask Henry for anything more than he'd already given her. She didn't want to get too consumed by her thoughts, so she gave him watering instructions instead. As she wiped the soil from her hands, she explained that a garden was easy to care for. Plants needed water and sunlight, and the clearing provided more than adequate sunshine throughout the day.

After the seeds were secure in the earth, covered with water, and warm from the midday sun, Henry led Rain a little deeper into the house to a door that had been closed when she first arrived at this cabin what seemed like ages ago.

He pushed the door open ahead of her to reveal a bathroom, so she could get cleaned up. In an effort that took more time than she'd realized, he heated large pots of water, filling the tub for her while she sat next to it on a small stool. When he was done, he turned to leave, but her fingers encircled his wrist before he could exit the bathroom.

"Henry?"

She didn't let go of his wrist and instead moved her hand into his, as he turned to face her. His eyes focused on her like nothing else existed in the world, and she almost forgot what she wanted to ask him.

Trying to regain her composure, she stole a glance at her ankle. "Can you help me . . . wrap this when I'm finished?"

"Yes, of course." His voice did not waver.

"Thank you."

He moved away from her then, though she had to force herself to let go of him, holding his hand as long as she could until he was too far away. He closed the door behind him, not looking back when he did.

She peeled off her dirty clothes and tossed them in a pile in the bathroom corner, then unwound her ankle dressing. Though it was the first time she'd ever been in here, she never thought a bathroom would leave her awestruck.

Like the rest of the cabin, it had a high ceiling with an angled skylight surrounded by natural wood beams.

Whoever had built this cabin had a particular

affinity for skylights as almost every room she'd been in had one.

The toilet had been removed from this room, or maybe there'd never been one to begin with because the fancy outhouse took that dirty job out of the cabin.

The colors surrounding her were all earth tones offset by white. The enormous white claw-foot tub didn't look antique but more like a much larger modern replica. She could swim around in there if she wanted.

A corrugated metal sheet curved around the other corner, extending well into the bathroom itself, making an open shower. Above that hung a matte silver waterfall shower-head which didn't matter much in the absence of running water.

Next to the shower stood a white pillar-basin sink with an oval mirror suspended by a braided wire. Rain hobbled over to it, and bracing herself, looked in the mirror.

Her hair stuck out in every direction, a tangled, filthy mess. She never knew how to describe her natural hair color. Cool ash brown? Regardless, she never liked it and had spent many years and a lot of money turning it into lovely shades of caramel.

These days, however, hair dyeing was no longer a priority, much less a possibility. Over the years her hair had grown and grown, and as often as she could, she snipped off the ends or had someone else do it until the caramel had disappeared. Now the awful brown color stared back at her in the mirror.

She pushed her hair away from her face. Fine lines had started to form under her eyes, masked a little by the dark circles that had also taken up residence there.

There'd been a time, most of her life if she'd been honest with herself, that body image issues plagued her. As she got older, however, she'd learned to love her body, pretty pleased with everything these days, despite her age.

Still it was hard to forget the days the media blasted messages that said women needed huge boobs and a tiny waist to be sexy, and no one was more relieved than Rain when the TV signals went dead. Today, Rain felt proud of her large hips, quads, and ass built strong over the past few years.

Rain decided she'd had enough ogling the mirror and dragged herself over to the shower area, plopping down on the small stool again. Henry explained she could clean the dirt and grime off herself here before relaxing in the tub, and he'd put down a large bucket of steaming water next to the stool.

He'd left her a washcloth, and there was even sweet-smelling soap, shampoo, and conditioner in the bathroom too. Of course, Henry had probably been living this way long enough to do things properly, so the amenities shouldn't have surprised her.

She soaped up the cloth after drenching it in the bucket and scrubbed the garden dirt off her skin until it was red. This bath had been the first time she'd gotten cleaned up since arriving at Henry's cabin, which must have been more than a week ago, and it felt better than any time she had ever spent getting clean in her entire life. Soapy and scoured raw, she doused herself with the remaining water in the bucket which gave her a shiver.

Fresh and clean, she sunk into the tub, the warm water flowing over her body. She eased her ankle in, watching the water plop over it, and immediate relief overcame her. Feeling more relaxed than she had ever felt since before the world went to shit, she put a water-soaked cloth over her eyes and dozed off.

Even though the better part of the day had been spent gardening and soaking in the tub, it still surprised Rain when she awoke shrouded in darkness. She felt like she'd fallen into an icy lake, so she scurried out of there as fast as someone recovering from an injury could move.

When her eyes adjusted, she wrapped herself in one of the large fluffy towels on a shelf near the sink. Since Rain wasn't very tall, it fell like a gown on her. Unfortunately, that gown was now her only clothing as the dirt-caked clothes she'd piled on the bathroom floor were all the clothes she possessed since she'd lost her pack somewhere in the woods. Not about to tarnish a super clean body with funky-smelling clothes, she dragged herself out into the great room where Henry sat reading by the fire, the walls dancing in an orange light show.

"Hi." Rain shuffled on her feet, trying not to put too much pressure on her injury, while adjusting her towel.

"Hi," he said.

"Um . . . I don't have any clean clothes."

"Right. Please sit. I'll bring you some of mine."

Rain breathed out a small sigh, as she slumped into one of the lush chairs. Henry disappeared into the bedroom and returned with a well-worn t-shirt and some extra-soft sweatpants. He handed them to her and then situated himself on the floor. Facing her, he began to wrap her ankle with a fresh dressing. Like always, he touched her with a gentle hand, while he made sure her ankle was mummified.

"There," he said. "It's bedtime. I'll give you some privacy to get dressed. Don't stay up too late."

"Thank you, H."

She watched him vanish into the bedroom but noticed he left the door open a crack. As she listened to Henry flopping around on the bed, she dropped the towel onto the table and struggled into the pants but had no trouble with the shirt. She collapsed onto her makeshift sofa bed and elevated her ankle.

"I love you! Sleep well!" Henry's shout from the bedroom almost caused her to fall off the sofa.

She blinked through surprise, but his tone had been playful and friendly, not laced with a bold expression of love at first sight.

"I love you, too!"

After that profession of appreciation, she never felt like hugging someone more than in that moment but decided to respect his wish for sleep rather than show up in his face demanding hugs. A short time passed, and she could hear no more noise or movement from the bedroom, so she figured sleep had taken him.

Not feeling even a hint of exhaustion herself, Rain stared at the skylight above the sofa for a long time. The thing she loved most about full dark was that the stars shone the brightest during those times. They glittered like diamonds thrown haphazardly above the cabin. As a shooting star streaked across the sky, she wished she'd heal a little slower, so she wouldn't have to leave Henry anytime soon.

3 CHICKPEA CURRY

THE REMAINDER of the month passed quickly for Rain and Henry. Their days consisted of Henry splitting logs for the fireplace and Rain pulling out tiny plants that had grown in too close, leaving room for the larger sprouts to grow.

Once in a while, while positioning a piece of wood to chop, he'd look over at her and raise his eyebrows toward the sky with a warm smile spread across his face. The first time he did this, Rain saw a face full of kindness, and Henry's attractiveness metaphorically slapped her in the face. Sharp angular features surrounded a significant nose, and his shoulder-length golden bronze hair flowed in whatever direction the wind wanted it to. However, his smile seemed to mask something deeper in him like a puzzle she couldn't seem to piece together.

Observing those thick eyebrows and his strong shoulders that rippled as he worked, Rain felt herself drowning in lust. Her heart drummed against her ribs, but she darted her eyes to the garden. Pushing soil around mindlessly, she feared she'd reveal her desires too soon, and like many past relationships they wouldn't be reciprocated.

The more moments that passed with him in the cabin, the more she yearned to be tangled with him under the covers. Her body often prickled with sweat as she spoke to him, and there were times she couldn't even remember what she'd said. She couldn't say why she felt this way nor why it consumed her. His smile always seemed to beckon her, drilling deep into her soul, and she thought she wanted him to penetrate her in other ways too.

About a month after Rain had arrived at the cabin, Henry disappeared in the middle of the night. She'd awoken, her throat feeling like sandpaper, and when she walked past his bedroom, she glanced in the wide-open door to find only a tangle of sheets.

Nothing in the cabin lay broken or had been jarred out of place, and she could see no blood anywhere. Nor did she find a note. No indication Henry had gone for a midnight stroll and would be back before she awoke.

The rational part of her brain told her to wait

for a few hours to see if Henry would stroll through the door like nothing unusual had happened. However, night dragged on as her eyes darted from the skylight to the front door.

The cabin remained in its same undisturbed state. Time's movement felt like trying to push a giant boulder up a hill, but then that boulder reached the top, and the sun shot up into the sky, rolling the boulder down the other side, revealing the cabin aglow with the morning light draped across the floor. Rain hadn't slept. Henry hadn't returned.

Panic crept into her stomach, and tears pricked the corners of her eyes. With Henry, she'd felt a sense of normalcy in her life that she'd lacked for a long time. The past month's new normal, the routine built with Henry, she'd grown to love. Heavy with worry, she feared she would never know normal again. With Henry now gone, she dreaded having to get back on the road to meet Dan.

Trying to distract herself, so she didn't have to make a decision to leave, she piled two fresh logs in the fireplace, her nose tingling with the rich musk of the wood. They caught with the help of some kindling. Throughout the day, she didn't add any new logs. Nor did she reach a conclusion about her future in the cabin.

The world was unpredictable, and being alone in an area she wasn't familiar with made her feel unsafe. Even though she knew for certain that she'd be safe with Dan, she wasn't ready to give up on Henry yet.

Night blanketed the cabin in darkness, and she watched the last of the red glow in the fireplace blink out. Then, she crawled into Henry's bed, the bedding still full of his scent. Cocooning herself in a blanket, she sobbed herself to sleep. In the night, the stillness inside the cabin and the quiet unknown outside filled her with terror. She flopped, a fish out of water, her mind a menagerie of her worst fears.

On the second night, she did the same, wrapping herself tight like a burrito in Henry's bed. The most prominent fear that buried itself behind her eyes was that he wouldn't return. Thoughts of abandonment did a cruel dance in her head. Then she reasoned he must be dead, which would explain his lengthy absence.

Nonetheless, the fear that they'd never spend another quiet night chatting by the fire cut through her. Her heart rapid with panic, drew up tears again, and she plunged her face into those pillows still covered with his smell, the smell she would never experience again. She couldn't stay here, but she made no move to leave.

The nightmares grew worse. She dreamed Henry had been taken from her, dragged bloody out of the cabin by a pack of wolves foaming at the mouth, their jaws crimson from a fresh kill.

The animals had Henry boxed in on all sides and leapt on him, all at once, tearing his flesh to pieces.

Rain awoke with a yelp, her back wet with sweat and face streaked with tears. She climbed out of the bed and fumbled into the kitchen. Shaking, she poured herself some water and tried to choke it down. Most of it ended up down the drain. She couldn't stop trembling and couldn't convince her brain Henry was anything other than dead.

The third day, depleted of energy, her body refused to move, but she couldn't bring herself to even nibble on something. She laid there motionless, her eyes moving between the window and the bag she'd packed and placed by the front door.

She watched ominous clouds blossoming near the mountains that rose high into the eastern sky. She put a pillow over her head not wanting to hear the thunder in the distance or the pattering on the roof when the rain arrived.

The thought of experiencing things without Henry settled on her like a weight. Without Henry, now she truly had nothing. She had nothing before Henry, only the promise of protection from Dan, a man she no longer loved. With Henry, the hope of something had bloomed. She lost hope, the more moments that passed without him and decided to leave as soon as the storm cleared.

A crash of thunder boomed throughout the cabin, and at the tail end of it, Rain heard another noise. It sounded like someone or something tromping up the porch steps on uneven legs. Shaking the clouds out of her head, she darted for the shotgun, even though she had no idea how to shoot it. Inching closer, a faint sound, like claws on tree bark, on the lower part of the door filled her ears.

Had some animal gotten up onto the porch? They were in a forest clearing after all, and wild animals were more abundant than ever before. Stranger things had happened. If nothing else, she could shoo the animal away from the house, so she unlatched and pulled the door open a crack which exposed human fingers the color of blood. A gasp got stuck in her throat, and she pushed the door, but it stopped moving when the slap of a palm hit it.

"Rain . . ." Henry's voice filled the space, tiny and weak.

She flung the door open but jumped back when she fixed her eyes on him. Henry was a crumpled mess and sticky with blood. She couldn't discern if he was injured or not.

If that initial shock hadn't rattled her enough, he wasn't wearing a single piece of clothing. His kind eyes, so glassy blue, burned deep into Rain, and they were reassuring yet at the same time terrifying.

"It's . . . not . . . my blood," he said, as if reading her mind.

While her feet wanted to take a step, her brain said to wait. If he was bitten or scratched, she'd have to kill him. Hesitation stood between them for a long moment before she decided. He had trusted her when she showed up bleeding on his porch. It would only be fair to extend that same trust back to him.

Finally, she set the shotgun against the wall and in that same movement dropped to her knees to meet him. Summoning great strength, she pulled his body close to hers and over the threshold of the cabin. Once inside, she slammed the door.

Rain hoisted Henry up and led him to the bathroom where he braced himself onto her as he climbed into the large clawfoot tub. Slumping forward, he pressed his forehead against the side of the tub, and she ran out to the back to fill two buckets of water from the well.

When Rain returned with the water, she hovered in the doorway of the bathroom. "Do you want me to heat some of this? It's really cold."

"I can take it," he said, extending his arm toward her. "Just come back to me."

Rain did as he asked and began to soap up a cloth. After her hands disappeared into foamy bubbles, she began to scrub. Removing layers of blood revealed purple bruises all over his body. Had he been in a fight? Based on what he'd said before, an opponent's blood had painted Henry's skin red. Had he killed someone?

The air was oppressive with silence. Henry, weak and pale from exhaustion, didn't move as Rain caressed his body with soap until she uncovered the man she had grown so fond of under all that blood.

Once clean and draped with a towel, Rain helped Henry into his bed. She didn't bother to try to clothe him, only covered his body with a sheet allowing him what little amount of decency she could give. He must have been anxious to sleep, so she made her footfalls as quiet as possible as she moved to the door.

"Rain . . . " He breathed her name in a whisper, stopping her in the doorway. "Come back, please."

Rain moved back to the bed sitting as light as a feather so as not to upset the mattress too much. She rested her hand on the bed next to her, and Henry reached over and gripped her hand in his. Her heart tried to beat out of her chest. Rain could think of nothing else but that she wanted Henry to wrap his hand around hers as often as possible.

"Will you," he said, pushing the words out with effort. "Will you hold me?"

Rain hadn't noticed she'd been holding her breath, and when Henry said that she puffed out a soft sigh of relief, as if she had been waiting for him to say this very thing for an eternity.

"I will never not," she said, her voice soft and gentle.

She slid down next to him in the sheets and pulled his body into hers, trying not to put any unnecessary pressure on his injuries. He rested his head on her chest, and she cradled him there. His body was ablaze with warmth, and she could almost see the heat coming off him in waves.

She stroked his hair, sometimes brushing his neck with her fingers. Henry sighed, and she could probably say that in this moment they both finally felt a peace neither one had known since before he had left her three days ago.

"H, you don't have to now, but someday you need to tell me what happened."

Henry nodded. "I need . . . I need you."

She did not release her hold on him. Nightfall took them deep into the heart of sleep and dreams which morphed into nightmares. Henry shifted around on the bed nonstop throughout the night, but he would always claw his way back into Rain's arms. This shook her the first time it happened, but she soon came to expect it, and each time she welcomed him back into her embrace.

In the morning the sun's rays peeking

through the windows pulled Rain out of sleep. Henry, who had previously told Rain he had always been a morning person, buried himself in the covers and refused to move. Throughout the day, Rain wandered around the house looking for ways to keep herself busy.

Around lunchtime she popped open a can of chickpeas and a can of coconut milk. She moved her nose toward the can, hoping to inhale the rich smell of the milk, but it seemed to have lost some of its potency.

Pushing around bottles in the pantry, she came across a bottle of dried garlic and onion and attempted to breathe life into them by soaking them in some oil. Once they somewhat resembled fresh vegetables, she set them sizzling in a pan with some curry powder and salt.

After they were bubbly with oil while the deep curry smell drifted around the kitchen, she poured in the chickpeas and the coconut milk. The curry simmered for a while until most of the liquid had cooked off, so she made it a bit more soupy by adding a little water. The smells that now wafted through the cabin caused a wave of relaxation to rush over her.

To end her creation, she added in a lucky find from the pantry, a snack size box of raisins. It didn't matter that the raisins had fossilized, cooking them would bring them back to life. The dry rice she also found there would make a perfect accompaniment.

While the rice was cooking and the curry bubbled away, she went to work inspecting the contents of the cabinets. It had been a while since she had tasted any alcohol, and she craved it in her bones. She opened every single cabinet in the kitchen, and their insides stared at her like a scene from a ghost story. No alcohol. Not even a bottle that contained fumes.

Her mind landed back on Henry while she finished cooking, and she heaped a too-large portion of curry over the rice and set it on his bedside table without a sound. She popped in and out of his room, and at dinner time swapped out an empty plate for one covered with more food. Though his belly was full, he never got out of bed.

While he holed up in the bedroom, she unpacked the bag she'd set by the door. Taking care of Henry had become a priority now. Dan would have to wait.

When night fell Rain again found herself lingering in the bedroom doorway, watching Henry sleep. He'd flopped onto his stomach with one knee up, the covers balled at the foot of the bed. Remembering that he was naked, she tried not to stare too long at his uncovered backside. However, this was silly because he hadn't been clothed when they had their arms around each other last night.

Her thoughts became ravenous, overcome with what would've happened if she hadn't been wearing clothes. Would anything have happened? Henry hadn't even hinted he had any feelings for her, and she told herself that his behavior last night was due to his weakness and vulnerability, not his need for Rain.

Now as her eyes traveled over the bruises on his back, she really needed to know what had happened to him in those two days. Who hurt him? What happened to the other guy? Was he worse off? Dead? She couldn't pull her gaze away from him as he slept. A wave of relief overcame her at the certainty that Henry was back, but she couldn't help but wonder . . . was he okay?

4 A Healthy Summer Salad

W HEN RAIN WALKED by Henry's room the next morning, she couldn't stop the voyeur in her from looking in. His naked back to the wide open door, she caught sight of him pulling a shirt over his head, and she almost let out a loud gasp.

It hadn't been the sight of his shoulders which looked like they had been chiseled out of marble that gave her pause. No, not the shoulders. She'd washed Henry just two days ago and slept next to him at night. She'd seen his back patchy with bruises. Bruises which should have been turning from purple to green by now. Now she'd seen no such thing. Nothing. His back looked smooth and clean as if he'd never been injured at all.

When he spun around to face her, she tried

to act like he hadn't just caught her with her hand in the cookie jar.

"Good morning." His voice flowed through the air with an evenness she couldn't even begin to match.

"Oh . . . hey." She silently cursed herself for sounding so shaky, shattering any illusion she'd been fine with what she'd seen.

If he noticed the apprehension in her tone, he didn't say anything. "How's your ankle?"

"Look at this!" Rain took a few unencumbered steps, twirled around on her good ankle as an added precaution, and then gave an exaggerated sweeping bow.

"Nice." Henry said, offering her performance a slight smile. "I'm going out to look for food today. Would you care to join me? Only if you think you're able to walk for a while."

"And if I can't? Will you carry me?" She fluttered her eyelashes at him, taking a step in his direction.

It did not have the reaction she'd hoped for as he took a few steps away from her, mumbling about his hair band as if he'd lost the most important thing in the world to him. When he finally found it and secured his hair back, he looked at her expectantly.

"I'm serious, Rain. I can do it by myself if you don't feel up to it."

"I'll be fine, H. I'd like to get out of here for a while, breathe in some fresh air, you know."

It was early enough in the morning that Rain didn't feel guilty for stopping on their walk more than she'd thought she would. Henry had nothing but patience, never once complaining about the frequent breaks.

As they trudged on, Henry promised Rain a serious rest at their first stop. Coming to a stop at a row of houses at the foot of a mountain made Rain wonder how far they'd traveled. She tried to conceal her surprise when Henry pried open what appeared to be a cellar rusted after years of abandonment. While she hadn't tried it herself, it looked like the contents of this cellar were doomed to be locked away forever. Yet, Henry flung the door open like it was brand new.

"Wait here a moment." Henry said, climbing down into the cellar. "I'll see if it's safe."

"Okay." Rain plopped herself down in the grass, happy to have at least a moment of rest.

She'd just gotten somewhat comfortable when Henry's voice traveled back up to her. "All good."

But she didn't even have time to proceed down into the cellar before he appeared, meeting her at the top of the stairs, taking her hand, and drawing her down with him. At the bottom step, her foot hit something jagged, and she tumbled into Henry.

He caught her before she smashed her head into the hard concrete floor. "I got you."

"Oh . . . thanks." Rain's breath came out ragged, and her heart pounded.

Henry held her there a moment until her breathing steadied. When it did, she swore he looked at her like he wanted to devour her lips, and she almost closed her eyes in anticipation of a kiss.

Instead he shoved her away, with perhaps a bit too much force, dusting the tops of her shoulders. "You okay?"

"Yeah, I'm fine." Her laugh bubbled out, more nerves than anything else.

Sooner or later she'd have to face facts. Holding Henry in bed after he'd been injured had been a one-time-only deal. A moment of weakness.

From what she'd seen, even though Henry moved through the world as a kind and caring man, it didn't mean he had any feelings for her.

Things would unfold as they always had. She'd end up falling for someone who didn't feel the same way about her, and she turned her focus to the shelves to avoid the churning in her stomach that told her even with someone, she'd always be alone.

Dusty cans and jars lined the cellar shelves. Rain already imagined what she could make with the several cans of beans and vegetables she now put in her bag. But Henry found the real prize. In one corner of the cellar stood a refrigerator, long dead after the world had lost power more than a year ago. When Henry pried it open, he exposed not only an unusual number of spoiled milk cartons, but an unopened twenty-five pound bag of flour.

Rain's mouth dropped open upon laying eyes on the Holy Grail. She thought whoever had lived here had been a real intelligent person, securing this bag of flour in an airtight refrigerator where small animals couldn't gnaw their way through the bag, and taint the contents with their feces.

Flour meant bread and tortillas. It meant she could make comfort foods long since lost to the world. She ran to the refrigerator and tried to heft the bag of flour. Twenty-five pounds proved to be heavier than she thought. Tears stung her eyes.

"Can you carry this back?" She asked, eyes on Henry, begging him to say yes.

It didn't seem to take him as much effort to heft the bag up and shimmy it into his pack. After that, he put his pack back on. When he almost fell over, Rain rushed to catch him, but found him simply pretending, righting himself before toppling over.

After returning from "shopping," Rain spent some time in Henry's library running her eyes and fingers over spines of many historical fiction books mixed with history books. She frowned at this abhorrent method of organization.

In addition to the history books, she saw books about nature, edible plants, hiking, and household repairs. One particular shelf stood out to her as containing a number of books about wolves.

She pulled one called *A Field Guide to Wolves* and paged through it. It was a simple book with page-sized full-color photographs detailing the appearance of various kinds of wolves around the world. A small blurb, printed at the bottom of each photograph, explained that particular wolf's diet and behavior. Standing there reading, she couldn't put it down, so she moved to the sofa before consuming the entirety of it before dinner.

When Rain woke up in the morning Henry had disappeared again. Like last time, he was gone for three nights and almost four days. During that time Rain felt a strong urge to break things while crying. His lying by omission had made her feel like not like a friend at all. But she resolved to get to the bottom of this, and if he refused to tell her this time, she'd be gone before he could lie to her again.

One warm morning Henry returned unharmed, without a word of where he had been nor what he had been doing. At first, Rain didn't attempt to interrogate him regarding his whereabouts, hoping he'd volunteer the information, but he kept his lips tamped shut. He went back to work around the house and in the garden, now overflowing with explosions of lettuce leaves, as if nothing had happened.

In the bathroom Rain washed her face, scrubbing off the weight of her time alone and once clean, tried to put on her best casual face. Her attempt at a normal facade didn't last too long when she knocked a glass off the kitchen counter trying to pour some water.

The tinkling shatter sent Henry rushing to her side to help her clean it up, but she pushed him away from her with one hand. Taking her attention off the mess, she pressed her other hand into the glass, a jagged piece slicing into her finger. She collapsed to the floor and started to cry, but she knew it hadn't been from the cut. Henry lifted her onto the kitchen counter, bandaged up her finger, and she leaned into his chest and sobbed there until she could talk again.

Though her breathing came out unsteady, she had to tell him how she felt. "I didn't know where you were again! I didn't know what happened to you or if you had left for good."

"I'm sorry for that. Come sit down." He guided her around the broken glass on the floor and to the sofa. "I'll tell you. I'll tell you everything."

Rain took her pink handkerchief from the

table near the sofa, and wiped her face. Her breaths started to come out more evenly.

"I don't suppose that you'll believe me when I tell you this."

Rain blinked her red, watery eyes up at him. "Try me."

"Night and the full moon—," Henry stopped his words short.

Rain furrowed her brow.

"This sounds so ridiculous. I don't think I can tell you this."

Rain opened her mouth, but he put a finger gently on her lips.

"I need you to see something, and I need you to trust me. Do you trust me?"

Rain nodded. "Yeah."

"I can't show you now. However, I promise you. If you can wait about a month, you'll have the answer to your question."

After a small inner battle, Rain agreed, and to seal the deal, he pulled her into his arms in a warm embrace and caressed her hair.

That month seemed to pass slower than all the others. The lettuces and radishes blossomed causing a sea of green in front of the cabin, so Rain cut some of the tops off. She also picked some of the mini tomatoes which had turned bright red, and pulled the tiniest carrot from the ground. It ended up in about four slices, but paired with freshly washed greens, sliced radishes, and cherry tomatoes, she couldn't have wished for a more refreshing summer meal.

Before the world had gone to shit, Rain had never purchased salad dressing. She loved making her own. Since production ceased and things were no longer mass-produced, she didn't have to worry about the bottled dressing that never tasted right.

She pulled balsamic vinegar, oil, and an unopened bottle of spicy mustard from the pantry. A proper dressing didn't just consist of vinegar and oil and spices. In order for it to fully come together it needed a binder or emulsifier. She whisked the mustard into the other ingredients forming a fully-blended, tasty salad dressing.

Crunching on fresh vegetables for lunch couldn't distract Rain from wondering about Henry's secret, and Henry also carried around a look of concern regarding something he swore could only be done via a visual confession.

Weeks before the full moon Henry brought Rain outside during the hottest part of the day and taught her how to shoot the shotgun. She'd fired a handgun before but never a shotgun. As the days passed, she learned to hit the targets he'd set up with better accuracy. He assured her no matter where she shot as long as she hit her target, it would surely die. She looked at him with a question behind her eyes, but she'd promised to trust Henry to explain to her what had been going on.

The night before the full moon, Henry showed her two places where he kept shotgun shells. Some he'd stored in the bedroom closet on a shelf too high for Rain to see. She climbed up on a chair, and her eyes moved over countless boxes of shotgun shells. She didn't ask why he had so many.

The other shells were hidden in a small cubby notched into the wall by the bowl of the kitchen sink cabinet. Unlike the shells on the shelf and the ones he had loaded into the gun earlier that day, these shells had blue casings instead of red ones.

He held them in his hands and said, "You need to use these special shells while I'm away."

"Why?"

"The other ones won't work," he said, his voice firm.

"Okay," she said, raising one eyebrow.

"Trust me. It'll make sense after what I'm about to show you. Your safety depends on it."

The first day of the full moon came, and Henry embraced her more times than she'd hoped for. When the sun began to sink toward the horizon, he checked the shotgun again to make sure it was loaded. He passed it to her.

"Remember what I said before," his voice

almost a whisper. "Point it directly at me. Any hit will be lethal."

Henry moved into the clearing away from the cabin, leaving Rain standing on the porch and about to start scratching her head. When the full moon started to rise, like a beacon it gave light where there had previously been none.

Henry let out a yelp followed by what sounded like a howl and doubled over as if in pain. She started to move as if to run toward him, but he raised his head and shouted at her.

"Stay there!"

These were the last words Henry uttered. His hair flopped over covering the front of his face, and she could only see the top of his head. When he raised his head, his beautiful blue eyes were gone and in their place two golden animal eyes with their pupils transformed into black slivers. They bore into Rain. His nails began to grow into claws which he used to rip off his shirt and the remainder of his clothes.

She stared in disbelief and horror at the change right before her eyes. The hair on his arms started to grow in thicker, and his chest sprouted hair where there had been none before. A small patch of hair turned into a thicket. His hands and feet began to elongate.

Henry howled like he was in pain, and Rain could see his teeth form into sharp points, with two daggers protruding forth. His already prominent nose moved three dimensionally from his face, becoming more and more snout-like.

Rain began to tremble, and with unsteady hands, managed to raise the shotgun and point it at Henry like he'd told her to. She felt sick at the thought of having to shoot him, but she didn't do anything beyond aim. She had no desire to kill Henry.

The transformation complete, the creature formerly known as Henry let out a rumbling growl, baring his new set of extra-sharp teeth, complete with fangs, before he pointed his muzzle skyward and howled.

He looked not at all anthropomorphic but rather like an enormous version of a Eurasian wolf. He began a shake that started at his head and traveled down his velutinous coat to his tail.

Henry's shoulder length blonde hair had fused at the neck with his newly emerged body hair, and now covered him in shining dark golden waves, streaked with black, and his snout and ears were dusted with white fur.

Rain could do nothing but stare. A shiver of fear overcame her and mixed with amazement, making her feel weird. She thought if the creature were to rise up onto its hind legs, it would tower over her.

Her hands still shook holding the shotgun, but she tried to hold it steady, keeping it fixed on him. She hoped muscle memory wouldn't fail her now.

The creature narrowed its eyes at Rain. He took a step and then focused his attention on the shotgun pointed at him. In this new form, Henry seemed to possess the same level of intelligence. She could see he recognized the gun, what it was loaded with, and that it could kill him. His front lips curled into a snarl, and then he turned and fled into the woods.

Rain blew all the air out of her lungs. She stopped shaking long enough to run back inside and barricade the door, feeling relieved they'd walked around the house early that day and closed all the windows.

Her feet took her all the way into the bedroom in the back, and she draped a blanket over her head as if it might protect her from all the scary things in the world. She did not cry.

Throughout the night, she gripped the shotgun until her fingers went numb and kept one hand on it at all times for the remaining three days.

Henry returned in human form, not even a scratch on his body. Rain didn't know where he'd gone but didn't feel like now was the time to ask that question. Other things weighed on them now.

Rain still had her hand on the shotgun. Henry moved toward her, and her heart beat as if a feral beast approached her. He didn't get too close, but she still took a step back when he took a step forward. He stopped moving as if waiting for her to say something first.

"How . . . " The words stuck in her throat, so she swallowed and tried again. "You're a wolf! How long have you been a wolf?"

She remembered she hadn't known Henry long, only a few months.

"Quite a long time." His tone sounded like someone dictating a shopping list.

He offered no further information. However, she refused to accept it this time, and her eyes bore into him, demanding more.

"Long enough for me to figure out that silver is lethal. That's why I gave you the blue shells."

"Does it hurt you? I mean, you looked like you were in pain."

"It does but not in the way you're thinking. After I change back, my muscles are sore, very much like after a workout."

"Have you killed people?" Rain whispered.

"I have, but I try not to kill unless it's necessary."

Her thoughts were jumbled together. Linear thinking had become an impossibility.

She thought about the shells again, "You said silver, right? We knew it killed them, but didn't really understand why."

"Basically, silver poisons us, and we react to it

like a person who had accidentally ingested dangerous chemicals," he said.

"Is that where you go when you disappear? To be with others like you?" She could feel the irritation spread across her face.

"I had in the past, but the last two months I left to protect you, from me."

Henry took another step closer to Rain. She did not take her hand off the shotgun.

"I need to know." He stretched his hand out to her. "I need to know if you're okay with this."

In the time she had known Henry, she had never been afraid of him until the night he became something everyone had feared for years. That terror didn't leave her; instead it settled on her shoulders like a heavy coat.

She wanted to reach out for his hand. She wanted to feel the warmth of his body next to hers, but she was still frightened. Her fears needed to enter the conversation.

"H, seeing you change like that scared me more than anything has my entire life, and I've watched presidential election results come in."

"You're funny." He coughed out a small laugh.

"Yeah, but looks aren't everything." Humor started to make her feel more at ease.

The tension in the room lifted. And she finally lowered the shotgun. She stepped closer to embrace him; neither moved to be the one to pull away. As he held tight for a long time, fear started to give way to hope.

They were locked in this embrace for what seemed like an eternity, and when they finally pulled away from each other he took hold of both her hands in his. His face clouded with seriousness.

"To be honest, I don't think I'm okay with this right now, but I care about you, and I want to be okay with it." Rain said. "Give me some time."

"I'm not going anywhere except during the full moon," Henry said.

Rain pulled her lips into a tight smile. "I know it's the middle of the day, but do you just want to lie around with me all day?"

"I'd love that," he said.

"One thing," said Rain. "What's that?"

"I want your arms around me."

"Yeah, I'll hold on to you."

5 Eggs Over White Beans & Spicy Tomatoes

SEEING Henry sitting across from her almost caused Rain to fall off the sofa. Last she knew, he'd excused himself to go to bed. But she guessed sometime early in the morning, he'd situated himself deep in the chair where he sat now with his hands on a book. Remembering how he held her the night before filled her with longing.

"Do you think it's ironic that the times we need the hugs the most are the times they're nowhere to be found?" Her voice startled him from his reading.

"Yeah, I think so." He folded his book over the arm of the chair. "Do you need a hug?"

"I feel like hugging you . . . since last night."

"I feel like being hugged." He got up, shimmied next to her on the sofa, and wrapped her in his arms.

When they'd talked about it last night, both Henry and Rain could describe themselves as people who loved hugs. Henry said he was more keen to hug people he cared about.

Prior to the world becoming a mess, Rain hugged people she felt a closeness or a connection to. She was drawn to Henry in particular because of the warmth he exuded. The feeling of Henry's warmth could best be described as moving into the bright sunshine after standing in the shade on a chilly morning. Her whole body was overcome with a feeling of instant gratification which flowed through her from head to toe.

"I wanna drown in your hugs." She put her face deep in his shirt.

"Good imagery." He pulled her tighter, locking her in his embrace for what felt like an infinite amount of time.

"How are you feeling?"

"Good. Hungry?"

"I'm always hungry."

He smiled and went into the kitchen. Rain listened to the crack of two eggs followed by sizzling in a pan. The sound of a can being popped open followed.

When he emerged from the kitchen with two plates in his hands, she saw he'd placed the eggs on top of two small hills of beans mixed with a can of spicy roasted tomatoes. Henry passed one plate to Rain and took the other for himself.

Before she ate, her eyes focused on him pulling hair band from his wrist and tying back his shoulder length hair.

"I'll be glad when more of those vegetables start to grow."

"Yeah." Despite everything that had happened Rain wanted to be around to see the rest of the garden bloom.

After they ate breakfast, Rain reclined on the sofa with a blanket draped across one leg. Henry sat cross-legged in the soft chair opposite her.

"Can I ask you something?" Henry said, filling the silence.

"Oh . . . sure," she said.

"Will you tell me about your life before I met you?"

Rain tossed the question around in her head like she was holding a hot potato. She generally didn't trust anyone. It was the way of the world: no trust here. That's how anyone survived.

But she'd trusted him to help her heal her body, and likewise she had taken care of him. Then he cared about her enough to share his secret with her, so after sitting on the question a moment, she decided to trust him with her mind too.

"I don't remember much of my childhood. My memory of it has always been fuzzy. I remember that my mother was usually an industrious and economical person while my father was cold and unkind. I had a brother too, but sadly I can't recall many times when I saw him happy. There was always so much hurt behind his eyes. It broke my heart. None of them survived when everything went to shit."

Henry looked at her as if there was nothing else in the room, but he didn't interrupt. His eyes begged her to continue.

"I always loved reading but never non-fiction. The real world is scary enough, you know. I love to draw, and for a while I was an event photographer, like parties and stuff. But I enjoyed taking pictures of anything. I think art became a way to express myself when I couldn't do it otherwise. I wanted to see beauty in everything."

"I like to draw too," Henry said.

"Oh yeah?"

"I like messy, sketchy stuff. Tight lines, not very refined."

"Awesome." Rain smiled.

"I'm really glad you came into my life, and I'm happy to learn about you. Tell me more."

"Okay, well, as long as I can remember, I've always been a people-pleaser. But I think I'm pretty unlucky in love. I wanted to be loved so badly that I would do anything to win someone's affection, but I often felt that no one ever loved me as much as I loved them. Most times this was true. After that, I got it stuck in my head that I must have done some really bad things, and I don't get to be happy in this life." Rain took a deep breath, feeling deflated.

"I think that's bullshit. You deserve to be happy." Henry's eyes, still focused on her, sparkled as he spoke.

A few tears escaped, and she pulled her sleeve across her cheek. Henry moved to the sofa next to her, and held his hand out to Rain. She rubbed her hand on her leg before inching it into his palm. Then, he drew her body into his and embraced her hard.

This is probably why she trusted him so much, the tender way he held her in his arms. He wrapped her with a concentrated effort to keep her safe and encircled her now as one would hold something precious with the utmost care.

Throughout her life Rain had tried to act like a badass to cover up how she sometimes felt fragile. With Henry's arms around her now, she kind of wanted to take on the world with him by her side.

He pulled away and looked at her, his face blanketed with seriousness. "You're enough."

"I haven't felt like enough for a long time," she said.

"You're always enough." He pulled her into his arms once again.

Time slowed. It was a while before he let her go, and when he did, he had that same serious look on his face as before.

"What is it you need from me?" He paused a moment. "From you, I like that you make me feel comfortable being myself."

She pursed her lips together, then smiled. "I need your kindness and warmth and your soft gentle spirit."

"I'm happy to share them with you."

"I like the way you make me feel." Rain rubbed her hands up and down her shoulders, as if trying to hug herself content.

"I like the way you make me feel too." He clasped her hand in his again, and it felt like putting her hand into a glove, a comfortable warmth. "Bonds formed by trauma are strong; plus if we're not 'ourselves' right now then we have more to learn about each other after some time."

They'd both had quite a bit of trauma in the short time they'd known each other. Even though they didn't quite know the extent of the other's pain, the state of the world offered little forgiveness, full of nothing except months and later, years of trauma. Too much time spent navigating the hardships of a society, a world in ruins.

For the first time Rain determined none of this mattered. Neither one of them could see the state of the world while they sat there talking to each other, their eyes only intent on what was in front of them.

Days passed this way, the two of them buried

in comfort, sharing stories. During his turn to share, Henry didn't say much about himself. He mentioned his father had been an abusive piece of shit and reflecting well on this man, stroking his ego, and letting him control his life as well as his sisters' lives was the only way to appease his dad. Like a weight had been taken off his back, he said he'd felt an immense sense of relief when his dad died.

His mother cameoed in conversation when he said he bore a resemblance to her. Henry said even less of his two sisters besides he thought them to be more outgoing than he was. Feeling abandoned, they were full of anger when he left home as the burden to care for aging parents fell on them. Used to being closed off and guarded, Henry said he didn't open like an unlocked door. Rain commiserated with him then because she saw so many parallels in their stories.

Her own father had been abusive and an alcoholic, which also gave her a tendency for alcoholism. When he drank, he broke things, and her mother had left him once when she and her brother were small, but her memory of this time was foggy.

Like Henry's sisters, Rain's brother stayed to care for their mother. Rain saw these threads connecting them, yet she could not celebrate them as joyful connections. The pain of the past, which sometimes seeped into the present, linked them.

Days of heavy unburdening left them exhausted, and when Rain slumped back into the sofa, Henry nuzzled next to her, resting his head on her shoulder. An immediate sense of relief settled on her then, and she couldn't recollect a time when anyone had made her feel this way.

Henry's demeanor washed with calm. Rain rested her hand on her thigh, and he reached toward her. When he laced his fingers in hers with a fluid and rapid movement, her heart fluttered.

She told herself it was ridiculous to act like a teenager with a crush. Nonetheless, she always felt a surge of emotions with Henry around. If Henry's feelings matched her own, it would be good, but if they didn't she'd be heading for a whole world of bad. If things went that way, she couldn't help but feel like maybe she deserved the hurt.

6 Fresh Baked Bread

AFTER THEY'D ACQUIRED the flour, Rain took a special interest in learning how to make bread over a fire. It took several tries and many failed batches of bread to perfect the recipe.

When Rain went digging through the cabinets one day, she found a Dutch oven. She'd meant to ask Henry if it came with the cabin or what. The Dutch oven served as a perfect makeshift oven because Rain found she could place another smaller pot inside of it.

Trial and error taught her that if she placed sticks in the bottom of the Dutch oven, it became more like an actual oven, circulating the heat and preventing the bottom of the bread from burning. Plenty of burnt bottoms later, she'd mastered this.

Putting the Dutch oven directly over the embers of the fire rather than suspending it worked better. By checking the loaf halfway through baking, she discerned that this method worked properly.

Hot coals over the top of the Dutch oven during baking would give the bread a more even color, brown on top and not burnt on the bottom because air flowed more freely.

During her time spent on the sofa, she'd seen a large hourglass encased in some kind of metal which had tarnished over time. Neither Henry nor Rain had bothered to try to polish or restore it, but it still measured what they assumed to be exactly an hour, perfect for measuring the length of time bread needed to bake over the fire.

The smell of freshly baked bread wafted through the cabin, as Rain set it to cool on the counter. When he came in from outside, Henry said he followed his nose in here. She slapped his hand away with a measure of playfulness when he reached for it. She distracted him by saying she wanted to go into town while it cooled.

As Henry and Rain stood staring down the length of the one main street, he dragged a frayed handkerchief across his brow. In the distance her eyes caught pops of color, and she took off on a slow jog toward the rainbow, stopping in front of a fabric store.

The shop itself had been mostly left alone as it didn't possess much of value beyond sharp objects. If she had to guess, Rain reckoned what remained of a diminished population valued survival over sewing. That or they didn't possess the particular know-how. The latter seemed more probable.

The shelves were empty of scissors, a huge loss as it made sewing more difficult, but she remembered seeing some back at the cabin, even if they weren't for cutting fabric.

"Did you know I can sew?" She moved through the store like a kid in a candy shop, her fingers falling on bolt after bolt of color.

"Like what?" He asked.

"Tops, dresses, anything really."

"That's really cool. You can make things that fit you perfectly. Which is your favorite of all the things you've made?"

Aside from needles and buttons, Rain started to fill her arms with a bounty of soft cottons in pinks, purples, greens, reds, and blues. "Oh probably any dress with pockets. All dresses should have pockets."

"Agreed." He held his arms out for more of the fabric she'd collected.

Rain unraveled two pieces of blue fabric flapping them out in front of Henry. "Which do you like better?"

"I like the one with the flowers," he said, pointing to a soft blue fabric dotted with tiny purple and pink flowers.

She tossed the plaid fabric away and added

Henry's choice to the stack. After that she climbed up on a shelf where rows of brand-new sewing machines in boxes sat gathering dust. Upon seeing the selection, Rain called to Henry asking for his help to bring back one of the sewing machines until she remembered there was no electricity anymore. Feeling pretty silly, she climbed down and shoved the fabric in her bag.

That week passed with Rain trying not to dwell on the sewing machine embarrassment. One morning Henry told her he was going "food shopping," but Rain, still feeling the sting of their last trip, opted to sit this one out. Instead she gave him a list of things she wanted including pickles, olives, wine and vodka for cooking, and sun-dried tomatoes in oil if he could find them.

Dusk crept in, and Rain found herself sipping hot tea by the crackling fire trying to read. When Henry returned, he beckoned Rain outside. She wrapped a blanket around her shoulders, following him outside.

He positioned himself in front of an object on the porch covered with a piece of cloth. She scrunched up her face until he pulled the cloth off in a dramatic sweep, exposing a very old sewing machine with a hand crank, requiring no electricity. Rain sucked in a gasp, her mouth a flat o.

"Where did you . . . does it work?" Her sentences jumbled together.

"It does," Henry said. "The crank is a little stiff, but I have some oil inside, and I'm sure it'll be good as new."

Rain dropped her blanket to embrace Henry, whispering endless "thank yous" into his ear. She couldn't seem to let go for a long time.

Back inside the cabin she set up a sewing table. Henry gave her some oil for the machine, which she poured into the gears until they moved.

The coordination to turn the crank and guide the fabric at the same time was not something she ever had a skill for. After what felt like hours of practicing, she had more crooked stitches than she knew what to do with.

Later in the evening Henry came to find Rain still at her sewing table. He stood behind her and put his arms on her shoulders, looking like his battery had run out.

"I need to sleep," he said. "Will you stay up much longer?"

"Maybe an hour or so. Go to bed. I'll go when I exhaust myself." She huffed out a little laugh.

He squeezed her shoulders gently. She grabbed his hand before he could walk too far away from her.

"Thank you for this . . . really," she said with a gentle squeeze.

"You're welcome." He returned the squeeze, smiling as he left her.

Rain stayed up for a while. In that time she'd gotten better but would need more practice before she could make something for Henry to repay him for this priceless gift. She thought about what she could do for him.

Rain's mother taught her to sew when she was a child, but it didn't stick and she gave it up to pursue other hobbies like reading vampire books or memorizing scenes from her favorite movies.

In her mid-twenties, Rain found her way back to sewing via a newfound love of vintage clothing, and she worked to learn the skill again, so she could have unique pieces of clothing.

Back then she made clothes exclusively for herself. Whenever someone asked her to make something for them, she refused. While she loved what came out of it, she considered sewing a chore, and didn't care to work for other people.

So she had no desire to make clothes for Henry, but she mulled over what simple thing she could make him that required much less effort than stitching together whole outfits.

When she had an idea of what to do, she was happy she had nothing else occupying her time, so she could devote herself to learning this machine. Less than a week later, she handed him a cloth tied with string.

"What's this?" he asked, all smiles.

"It's something for you."

He opened the cloth to reveal a pale blue handkerchief with tiny purple and pink flowers, the same fabric he'd picked out at the shop. When he held it up, she noticed that the blue matched his eyes, and even though all the stitches weren't straight, it was still better than the almost frayed to death handkerchief he had.

"You made this, didn't you?" he asked.

"You bet I did. I finally got a handle on the crank system. It's more difficult than an electric machine but not impossible to use. Anyway, it matches your eyes and will probably last a little longer with hemmed edges."

"I love it," he said, pulling her into his arms.

She melted in his arms, not wanting out of this embrace. Not this time. Not any time.

7 HENRY'S WORLD FAMOUS PB&Js

THE NEXT DAY, Henry danced around, shifting from foot to foot in front of Rain, looking like the weight of the world had settled onto him.

"I need to tell you something," Henry said. "It's only fair to you."

"I'll listen . . . to anything you have to say."

"I'm glad." Despite his simple answer, Henry breathed out a heavy sigh after it. "I don't know where to begin. There's so much to tell, and none of it is easy."

"I understand. Go at your own pace. I'm here, and I'm not going anywhere."

She put her hand out, and he wrapped his own hand around hers and led her to the sofa.

"I appreciate that. First, I need to tell you about Siobhan. She's a wolf like me. Before any of this happened we'd been together since high school, more than twenty years. She understands me better than anyone, knows all my flaws, my struggles, but also knows my strengths. Like you she's experienced the good things about me too. She's seen me at my best and my worst, always by my side for everything. She was always a huge pillar of emotional support for me. She was my partner."

Rain tried to hide the hurt that tumbled out with her words. "Okay, Henry, I get it, I mean, but if you have her, then why are you here with me?"

"About a year before I met you, I came to this cabin to escape an uncomfortable situation. Siobhan had become fixated on growing our pack and chose me as the wolf she wanted to mate with. But I didn't want this and, well, I ran away. I know it wasn't the best course of action, but Siobhan can be very controlling. She gets her way with me all the time even if it's something I don't want to do.

"Every full moon I used to travel back to the place where we had made our home and watch her. Not too long after that I found that she had replaced me. She had chosen a new breeding male, and they had a litter. She had a proper pack. I continued to spy on her for a while and watched the pups grow. Our kind has evolved, so we don't grow like humans but more like animals, meaning much faster.

"One day I was finally able to distance myself from her, to try to put an end to my obsession with her. But she knew I watched her. One day I stopped watching her, and she came for me here. I've chased her away from this cabin more than once. She can't handle me being enamored with anyone besides her."

"Did you become enamored with something else?" Rain asked.

"Yes."

"With what?"

Touching her face softly, Henry looked her straight in the eyes. "With you."

"I don't know if that's a good thing or a bad thing, H. I mean what if you get bored with me?"

"You're not like anyone I've ever met."

She let out a tiny laugh followed by a serious face. "I kind of pride myself on that."

"I know." Henry smiled. "And I love that about you."

Rain scrunched her forehead together. "Do you think she'll come back here?"

"Honestly, I don't know," Henry said. "I think she still wants me despite getting what she wanted from another wolf. We have a history, and I think that keeps nagging at her. It's quite possible she wants me as her subordinate male. It probably *really* bothers her that she doesn't have me to control anymore. But now that she has another breeding male, and I've expressed my firm desire not to be involved in mating with her, I'm not sure why she still wants me."

A rumbling came from Henry's stomach and Rain, feeling the same, put it into words. "I'm getting hungry."

"Let me make you a sandwich," Henry said.

"I'd like that."

Rain sliced four pieces of bread, and the simple act of pushing the knife through the bread seemed to lift her spirits. Bringing a playful mood back into the air, Henry boasted he could make the best peanut butter and jelly sandwiches in all the lands.

"Tell me something," Rain said. "What makes your PB&Js better than anyone else's?"

"I suppose it's the method," Henry said. "You can use the same knife, but make sure you clean it in between the jelly and the peanut butter."

At this, Henry spread a generous amount of jelly on one piece of bread, wiped the knife with his fingers and then licked the jelly off. A brief naughty image flashed through Rain's head, but she decided not to vocalize it.

"I used to teach children 'cooking' classes." Henry did actual air quotes. "I had to teach four-year-olds how to make peanut butter and jelly sandwiches. Nobody wanted to do the cooking classes because they thought they were shitty. I thought they were awesome. There were kids who came in who didn't wanna use the jelly, and

I was like 'no you can't do that you have to use both.'"

Rain laughed. "They just wanted a peanut butter sandwich."

"Yes, but I was pretty stern with them."

"Yeah, show those four-year-olds who's boss!"

"That's right. The best part was that I had to demonstrate how to make the sandwiches, which meant making them myself. So at the end of the day I always had sandwiches to take home." Henry spread much less peanut butter on the other half of the bread. "It wasn't so much that I made them any special way. I just learned to make them fast."

"Got it," she said.

He closed the sandwich, sliced it in half triangles, and handed it to her. "They're easier to hold this way."

"This makes me feel like a kid," Rain said, taking a bite.

"Eventually, I anticipate not being able to find peanut butter and jelly anymore, and that means my sandwich making days are over."

"Sad," said Rain. "It's funny how many things we took for granted before all this happened."

"I know. The things we never think about when we had modern conveniences."

They ate their sandwiches in silence with no more talk of Siobhan.

8 Simple Cabbage Soup

ALMOST THREE WEEKS before the next full moon, Rain made a crude calendar by drawing boxes in a notebook. She knew full moons happened about every twenty-eight days.

She marked in the notebook the day Henry had last disappeared and started counting the days with the rising and setting of the sun. Diligence became paramount because her survival depended on not crossing paths with wolf-Henry.

While she trusted him to disappear as he always had in the months before, she also felt like her safety depended on her ability to be as knowledgeable as she could about her current situation. Every morning when she woke up, she drew a square indicating another day.

Now weeks had passed and Rain stood staring out the window as afternoon sun warmed the clearing. Henry lounged on the sofa, feet up, book in hand.

"What should we do today?" She opened the window, letting the cool air in.

"What do you want to do?"

"Nothing in particular."

"Same."

"Actually, I want to braid your hair. I really do." Right after saying it, she thought maybe he'd wouldn't like that and felt silly for asking.

"I want you to," he said. "I like braids, and I like you."

"It's settled then." She moved to sit on the floor. "Come here."

With his back to her, he nestled in between her legs and leaned back. She wrapped her legs around him, pressing into his waist slightly.

"This feels nice," he said.

"You feel nice." She couldn't decide if she was joking or being lustful, but probably both.

She chatted with him about nothing in particular while she pulled strands of his shoulder length hair, one by one, into a French braid.

Their conversation evolved to "remember when," and she found herself drifting back to the times before these. Movies, TV shows, pop culture, memes. All long gone. All distant memories now. Remembering things people once deemed important but realizing they didn't exist now, always seemed kind of surreal.

When she finished, his hair was beautifully braided. She pulled the hair band off his wrist, which seemed to live there until he ate, and secured it at the bottom of the braid near the nape of his neck.

"I wish you could see it," she said with a twinge of sadness. "I learned to do this by practicing on myself. It wasn't too difficult."

He reached around his neck finding the tail and felt up the length of the braid. "Cool."

"Are you hungry?" she asked.

"A little. You?"

"Yeah, help me make us something."

They went out to the garden and came back inside with a small head of cabbage, carrots, an onion, and a head of garlic. When Rain cut into the onion the fumes swirled up into her nose and her eyes grew watery. The garlic canceled out the pungent onion as she breathed in its sharp smell while smashing it.

Henry set up a large pot over the firepit outside and added a little oil. Passing him the chopped onion, she told him to sizzle it until it softened. He pushed the pieces around the pot, making sure they didn't burn, and then she instructed him to add the garlic after the onion became golden.

Back in the kitchen, Rain squared the remainder of the vegetables before joining Henry outside once more. He'd handled the onion and garlic, so she dropped in the carrots, careful not to splash him with scalding hot oil. White beans, canned tomatoes, and a little water joined the soup next. Time and time again she found anything canned food swam in only helped amplify the flavor, so she always added their liquids.

Though often expired, dried herbs like thyme and oregano were still pretty easy to find as well as salt and pepper, so she seasoned everything with those. Rain smiled, grateful that even though a multitude of things had been taken away from her in this new world, cooking was still something she loved to do and helped pass the time.

She sliced the remainder of the bread, making a mental note to bake some more during the full moon, giving her something to do in Henry's absence. Cabbage soup finished, they sat on a blanket in front of the fire inside the house and ate picnic-style.

Later, deep into night Rain awoke to a bitter chill, so she got up and closed the window. When she walked past Henry's room, the oppressive emptiness of it stared back at her.

Because of the calendar she'd made, she knew a full moon would be here soon. She hadn't expected him to disappear in the middle of the night. But it made sense.

Henry had lived this way for a long time. He

had to possess a greater knowledge about the beast within and knew better than anyone the safest time to leave before he transformed. Rain noted this courtesy, this regard for her safety, as one more way Henry showed he cared about her.

When she returned to her bed on the sofa, her heart sank at the unmistakable sounds of claws clicking along the wooden porch. Scraping followed. Her hands shook as she wrapped them around the shotgun. She couldn't go out the front door because she knew a wolf was there, scratching to get in.

Her whole body trembled as she crept out the back door, around the side of the cabin, and almost came face- to-face with Henry. She knew it was him. She knew it. She recognized his unique coat even in the dark. But why hadn't he left?

A low growl bubbled out of his throat. She already had the shotgun on him as he took a step forward.

"Go away!" Though she'd tried to make it as loud as possible, she heard her voice shake.

The wolf remained still but growled louder this time, streams of saliva dripping from his fangs.

Tears burned her eyes, threatening to spill out in rivers, but she yelled louder. "Get the fuck out of here!"

Her hand felt numb from how hard she

gripped the shotgun, but the wolf snapped his mouth shut and leapt off the front porch before disappearing into the woods. She ran back inside, bolting the back door behind her.

Rain did not cry. Instead, she worked to steady her breathing, telling the tears "not today." Her hands still shook, and it felt like an eternity before she could let go of the shotgun.

When she stopped shaking, she felt a great sense of relief with him gone. The moon shone, a great lamp through the window. Even though all the windows were closed, a deep shiver penetrated her bones, so she grabbed the heavy blanket she had kicked off earlier and pulled it up to her neck.

The air was arctic. She missed Henry, the man. She missed the way his hand curled around hers and how her body molded into his whenever he enfolded her into a hug. The wolf she could definitely do without and heaved out a sharp breath of relief that the beast was gone, possessing no great desire to meet it again.

She dragged the heavy blanket into Henry's bed. She didn't leave the house for the next three days, hiding under the covers, sipping hot tea and trying not to let her fears get the better of her.

During the day, she found herself staring out the window, but at night closed the curtains tight, afraid that if she peeked out there, yellow eyes would be gazing back at her as if attempting to burn a hole through the glass.

When she slept, her dreams devolved into nightmares. She saw the wolf clawing open her chest and ripping out her throat. Coming in torrents, blood soaked her clothes.

Covered in sweat, her body on fire, Rain opened her eyes to Henry sitting on the edge of the bed holding a mug. Without thinking, she kicked herself away from him and huddled against the wall. The amber contents of the mug ended up everywhere.

"Fuck," he murmured.

He set the mug on the table, liquid spilling down its sides, and walked out of the bedroom. When he returned, he had a towel bunched in his hand. Rain still pressed her back against the wall, wrapped in the heavy blanket and shaking though the air had warmed. She tried to control her breathing.

After he finished mopping up the mess with the towel, he resumed his place on the bed and crossed his legs, resting his folded hands on his lap. Henry sat still and didn't move closer to her. He only looked at her with kind eyes, no malice or threat of any kind behind his gaze. Nonetheless, Rain remained a fixture on the wall.

"Are you okay?" He breathed out the question.

She inhaled sharply. "I had a nightmare."

"Do you want to talk about it?"

She pulled the blanket tighter around her and sat there feeling heavy for a long time. Henry's face read like he'd be content to sit in this silence as long as she needed him to. After some time she let go of the tension in her back and shoulders, relieved that the man she had come to know, the man who sat in front of her now, was still Henry after all.

She gathered her thoughts before speaking again. "In the dream, you . . . you killed me . . . and it was violent."

"Which me?" Henry asked.

"It was the wolf, but it was still you, you know. The creature looked exactly like you did the other night covered in blonde fur." She paused, time dragging by before she spoke again, her words coming out in sharp breaths. "I'm having a hard time with this to be honest. I'm really fucking scared."

"I get that," he said.

"I'm certain that I've never experienced anything like this before, and I had always felt safe with you . . . until the other night when you didn't leave."

"I understand," he said. "If it makes you feel better, while many things about this aspect of me are unpredictable, I have learned to control it to some extent."

"To what extent?" she asked, raising an eyebrow.

"Well, the animal does take over, but I'm still there inside. I can't control him completely, but I can push him a little bit."

"What does that mean?"

"It means I can urge him a little to make decisions either for or against something," Henry said. "However, I need to be honest with you. He's a very powerful, instinctual animal, and I'm not always successful."

"That's equal parts comforting and terrifying."

"I'm trying the best I can. I've been struggling with this beast almost my entire life."

"I know *Henry* wouldn't, but I'm afraid the animal will hurt me someday, especially after what happened on the porch."

"I don't want to hurt you."

"I know you don't. But I can think of a million ways for you to hurt me." When she said it, Rain didn't know if she meant physically or emotionally.

"I never want to hurt you." He punctuated the words as if indicating a truth he firmly believed.

She stared at him for a while, suddenly feeling incredibly cold again despite the growing warmth of the day. Inside her head she cursed the blanket for not doing its job properly.

"I'm still scared, H."

"I know. I won't push you. I know this is hard to accept and to be honest, I've never shared the wolf with anyone who wasn't like me. But you are comfortable to be around, and you care about me, so I trust you. Maybe that's why I stayed here instead of leaving like I always had before."

"That's all true. I hope . . . maybe being scared will pass or maybe it won't. Perhaps I'll always be scared of you. But I like the way you make me feel."

"I like the way you make me feel too," he said.

They didn't move from their respective sides of the bed, an ocean between them and more than that, a mountain to scale. Like any momentous task, Rain thought it best to slowly attempt to scale this mountain. She couldn't rush her feelings, but she reached out for Henry's hand then. The first step in a long journey.

Over the next few days Henry kept a physical distance from Rain. In turn, she found herself not jumping for affection like she always had. This dynamic shift caused an awkwardness to permeate the cabin.

She cared about Henry as a person, a loving and gentle man. He always took great care to be mindful of her physical and mental health. She wanted to be with Henry, to love him, but she knew loving a person meant loving them entirely in spite of their flaws.

Was the wolf a flaw? Or was he considered an intrinsic part of Henry, belonging to him as a complete person and something that could never be separated from the man? She reconciled, after much thought, it was the latter, and loving Henry meant loving both of them.

So then the question became: could she do that? Loving the man, easy. Loving the beast, an impossible task. They were not the same.

When he'd growled at her on the porch, Henry looked like an unpredictable and dangerous creature, capable of great violence. As a human, the man embodied the exact opposite: compassionate, controlled, and harmless. In her mind Henry now became a walking contradiction, something difficult to come to terms with. But she was known as a fighter, definitely where relationships were concerned.

Her mind wandered back to her last relationship. Before the apocalypse, before the wolves, she'd been with Dan. They were together for the better part of six years, and Rain had loved him enough to marry him.

Working through a tumultuous but not impossible relationship, they somehow managed to patch things up time and time again. However, over time he came to value work more than her. Work days extended later and later into the nights until he'd completely lost interest in her.

Much like the moon, his affection waned until it disappeared entirely.

At one point Dan and Rain were practically giddy discussing their plans to start a family. It seemed that fate favored them. Within six months of trying, Rain found herself staring in disbelief at a little plus sign. But before she could even go to the doctor for official confirmation, she started her period.

This was a minor catastrophe compared to what came next. Two years had passed since their early miscarriage. Despite being older, Rain had been taking better care of her health. Through dietary changes and regular exercise, she'd lost a significant amount of weight. Then it happened. She took pregnancy tests for a week straight, each one showing positive, and when they saw the tiny pulsating heartbeat on the ultrasound machine, Rain and Dan celebrated with genuine joy.

Yet nothing could sooth Rain. Her previous early miscarriage with Dan had not been her first. At twenty-one, a different story unfolded. Then she'd gotten pregnant not because she wanted to but because she and her boyfriend at the time were young and careless. Despite still feeling like a baby herself, she vowed to have the child and maybe they'd grow up together.

A doctor's appointment. A heartbeat. And twelve weeks. Until one evening she woke up in the deepest darkness of night in more pain than she'd ever felt in her life. There were a few times in her life she had crawled across the floor to her bathroom. This one, however, etched itself into her memory, a scar left for eternity.

As Dan and Rain looked at a clear healthy heartbeat, two miscarriages and advanced maternal age put Rain in a constant state of worry in regards to their baby, so she asked her doctor if she could visit the clinic as often as she could to monitor its growth. Seemingly sympathetic to Rain's unending fears, the doctor allowed her to come in for bi-weekly ultrasounds. Subsequent doctor's appointments continued to breathe relief into Dan and Rain's lives as their rainbow baby continued to grow.

Then a dark cloud put an end to the sunshine. At perhaps nine weeks, the doctor couldn't discern a heartbeat. That day the doctor's words were icy, emotionless, so Rain fired her doctor. A fraught-filled car ride the next day put Dan and Rain in a different doctor's office. The doctor confirmed that sometime around six or seven weeks the baby had stopped growing.

This devastating news was probably the catalyst that sparked the dissolution of their marriage. Dan drowned himself in work; Rain drowned herself in alcohol. Their shouting got louder.

Each fight uglier than the first with tears enough to fill oceans.

Rain spent her time with her friends drinking herself stupid every weekend. One night she drove home drunk at 4AM. She didn't care what happened to her, and her reckless behavior continued. Her husband no longer touched her anymore, and one day communication stopped altogether.

Monetarily Dan had always been kind to her. She didn't want for anything except for affection. Right before the world erupted into chaos, Rain decided to leave him. She bore no hate toward him, but being with him became too much to bear.

She fought for Dan and for their marriage non-stop until one day she couldn't fight anymore. Her body could no longer move in any direction that led to saving their relationship. They separated but remained cordial.

In her life, Rain had overcome three miscarriages, started anew after a failed marriage, and survived the apocalypse. Loving a wolf seemed like just one more hurdle to clear. She'd made her decision then. She hadn't quit her marriage when it had become difficult. She fought for Dan for as long as she possibly could.

Even though the situation with Henry was not the same, she had to fight for this too. She'd loved Dan once upon a time; she could love

Henry in another way, a different way, a better way.

So Henry was a wolf. It's not like he walked around the cabin thinking about murdering her, right? He'd only change, and hopefully fuck off, once a month. She could deal with this.

From the kitchen she eyed Henry sitting far away on the sofa. Rain walked over and put her hand out to him.

"Come here." She pulled Henry up into her arms and embraced him, feeling all the air escape his chest.

He spoke after some time. "Are you okay?"

"Maybe I'm not completely okay right now," she said. "But I care about you, and I will try to be okay with who you are . . . all of who you are."

"I'm glad. I'm sorry I was careless before."

"Yeah, I think that's about right."

"I know I ran off into the forest, but I could just as easily have not. I could have hurt you." He sat on the sofa with a heavy thud.

She sat down next to him and locked her fingers in his. "But you didn't, and I believe you must have been inside, pushing that creature, telling him not to hurt me. So I trust you, H."

He turned his head away from her, burying it in the pillow in the corner. She interpreted his body language as fleeting shame and felt pulled to him. She reached over his body in a backwards hug until he turned around and pulled her to his chest.

His warmth engulfed her as it radiated around her body, swallowing every ounce of cold she felt. She missed this all-consuming feeling of being in his arms and the total amnesia to the rest of the world it offered her.

"I'm glad you're back," she whispered.

"Me too," he said quietly.

9 Penne with Black Beans

FOUR WEEKS after they'd talked seriously, Henry disappeared and relief swam through Rain upon not finding him on the porch that evening. If she'd been honest with herself, she almost didn't want to check, afraid he might actually be there or that her mind tried to play tricks on her, conjuring up a wolf where there was none.

The first day of his absence Rain watched the clouds from afar as they curled in, dark and ominous. Soon those blackened rumbling rainclouds would climb over the mountaintops and drench the forest and clearing with rain.

Watching from the warmth of the cabin and listening to the thunder boom in the distance, she curled under a blanket. The only illumination came from the fire in the fireplace which set the main room ablaze in a tangerine-colored glow.

The only sounds were of the logs cracking and breaking apart. Rain didn't feel like moving.

She'd clamped the windows tight and secured all the doors. She still didn't feel quite safe alone, and the looming storm paralleled that inner turbulence.

Rain decided to make something simple to eat. Over the fire, she brought a pot of water to a rolling boil, and into that she plopped in some penne pasta, which didn't come out until al dente.

In a small separate pan she sizzled onions and garlic then dashed in herbs and salt and pepper. She then added a vibrant can of tomatoes, and black beans for contrast.

Even though this dish was packed with flavor, she nibbled on the pasta. She hadn't been bothered by hunger and preferred to share this meal with Henry.

Bored silly, Rain needed another distraction. Her eyes darted around the cabin desperate for something to keep her mind off Henry's absence. Another book? She doubted she could focus on the words on the page let alone the story. She eyed the gramophone, remembering when Henry showed it to her for the first time.

"It's a phonograph!" She clasped her hands over her mouth.

"Gramophone." Henry corrected her, emphasizing the precise word. "I found it while scavenging one day, brought it back here, and fixed it up. The records I've collected over the past year. That's why the selection is so varied. I just picked up every one I found."

"Show me how it works!" Her voice echoed through the cabin like a child with a new toy.

"It's quite easy. You just wind here." Henry gestured to the winding handle. "Soon you'll feel some resistance. That's how you'll know it's time to stop winding. Don't worry about winding it too much because if you tried, the resistance would prevent you from doing so."

Rain was enthralled. She never tired of listening to Henry's even and soothing voice, so pleasant to listen to.

"I love listening to your voice." She looked a bit sheepish, not meaning to vocalize her feelings in that moment.

He smiled. "That's so nice to hear. I've never been told I have a nice voice."

"It makes me feel so at ease all the time."

He pointed back to the gramophone. "Next you're going to release the brake, wait until the gramophone is at full speed, and then gently place the needle on the record."

"Do I need to wind it again?"

"No need," Henry said. "Fully wound it should play this entire side. I've done this many times. Music helps the quiet days go by faster and eases my mind when I'm feeling troubled."

"I remember how that felt. I miss it so much. It's amazing how still and quiet the world is without music in it. How empty."

"I get that."

"What do you say to lying on the sofa all day under blankets and just listening to music all day?" Rain asked.

"I would love that," Henry said.

"Perfect."

❧

Rain wished today was like that day had been: music drifting around the room, Rain and Henry under blankets on the sofa, a wonderful day. But Henry was the main thing missing from today, and the only thing that could kill her boredom.

Music, though, she could still have music. She chose a classical record. Light, soft, with no lyrics. She wound the gramophone like Henry had taught her, released the brake, and placed the needle.

She wanted sounds other than that awful storm as the rain started to fall. At first it sprinkled on the skylight, but it soon grew heavier until pouring from the sky. The melody from the gramophone flowed through the room where Rain sprawled on the sofa barricaded in the house.

But the music failed as a distraction as her mind seemed to return to Henry and his absence. She wanted to wrap him in a hug, rest her head on his chest, and listen to the soft thumping of his heart.

A peal of thunder boomed closer than before, and from the clouds burst forth another torrent of heavy rain. Rain frowned at those clouds for a moment before drawing the curtains with more force than necessary. She could shut the storm out of sight by closing the curtains, but couldn't cover the skylight. It looked like the wind- shield of a car going through a storm the way its slant caught the rain.

Rain got up to toss another log on the fire and put the kettle over it for more tea. She figured it wasn't very late, but she had a strong desire to be in bed soon to forget the plaguing loneliness. She decided to cocoon herself in a blanket soon as the gramophone continued to warble its classical tune throughout the house.

The next day as Rain wondered how she'd spend her remaining time alone, she remembered Henry had brought home some art supplies one day while scavenging. Both Henry and Rain expressed a particular interest in art. Though it seemed like a silly thing to do during these times, it brought them joy in a world where little was worth celebrating. Rain tried to find joy wherever she could.

She went digging around in the drawer where Henry had stored the supplies and produced a sketchbook. Flipping through the pages, she saw drawings of various animals: tons of birds, a fox, and goats. Just as he'd said, Henry had a rough sketchy style of drawing, hard lines carved into the paper. In contrast, Rain's lines bubbled and curved, and she took special care to clean the sharp edges.

Why had he never shown her these drawings before? She smiled and pressed the sketchbook to her chest. She wondered if she could recall Henry's face well enough to sketch him in an animated style, his lips locked with hers, his shoulder-length hair blown back by the wind.

In the midst of sketching out a face and hair, she heard a sudden, yet familiar, noise from outside. She grabbed the shotgun, peered out the window. A motorbike shredded through the grass and mud around the cabin. And when she saw the helmeted rider stop and park the bike in front of the cabin, she flung open the front door and walked toward the person, pointing the shotgun at them.

The rider shouted something muffled by the helmet before throwing an arm up in surrender.

Still aiming at the stranger, Rain said, "Yeah,

I can't hear you."

The rider pulled off the helmet. Rain squinted, but she didn't need to because without a doubt she recognized this tall, thin, dark-haired man. How could she not recognize someone she'd spent six years with?

"Dan," she whispered but couldn't force out any more words after that.

Dan advanced forward. "Rain!"

Rain did not lower the weapon. Instead, she shook her head in a "no" gesture and continued to point it at him. "Stay there! Don't you come any closer!"

"Rain, I am here to help you!" he said.

"I don't need your help anymore, Dan!"

Dan tried to protest, his voice taking on a slight whine. "This place is dangerous. There are wolves everywhere. One of our scouts killed one in the forest not too far from here. We think that there may be more of them. Come with me. I can protect you!"

Rain swallowed hard, forcing down a lump in her throat that surfaced when she feared his scouts had killed Henry. Tears threatened to erupt, but she fought them back with shaky breaths. A howl in the distance sliced the silence between them, and soon a second howl sounded even closer.

"Can you hear that?"

"I think the best thing is for you to get out of

here, Dan."

"I am not leaving without you," he said. "I have been looking for you for *months*. My friends and I were on the roof of one of the buildings in the town when we saw you. I wanted to approach, but you were not alone, and I was worried you might have been taken prisoner."

"Taken prisoner? Do you hear yourself? What is this, medieval times?"

"And then we followed you to the cabin of your jailer. I came back, hoping to find you alone, so I could rescue you."

"Well, all that was unnecessary. As you can see, I'm fine, not imprisoned. I'm fine, so I strongly suggest you get the fuck out of here before you get hurt."

Dan, stubborn since the day she met him, eyed her with an air of suspicion, but refused to move despite having a shotgun pointed at him. Her eyes traveled over him as well as the bike, but she could not discern any visible weapon.

"Rain, you are being stubborn! Please follow me now!"

"*I'm* being stubborn? You're the one being stubborn! I said I don't need your help anymore Dan!" She put more force, more seriousness behind her words this time.

At that moment a strong wind picked up and blew through the trees causing a fierce rustling sound to permeate the area. Rain shivered.

"Rain—," Dan started.

But Rain cut him off. "I'm not your fucking responsibility!"

The palpable tension in the air now mirrored their married life. Back then everything devolved into an argument, into screaming enough to rouse the neighbors. The painful, yet familiar, feeling swallowed her, and she hated it. Despite the peace being sucked out of the atmosphere, neither one of them moved.

"Don't make me repeat myself, Dan. I said get the fuck out of here!" Her voice reverberated against the trees.

Rain wasn't sure if the movement she saw in the brush had been the wind or something else. Did she imagine a tuft of blonde fur?

"You are going to get hurt, Rain."

She groaned in frustration. "We're talking in circles! This is so pointless! Please, fuck off."

The trees started to shake. Just the wind. Finally, much to her relief, Dan whipped one leg over the seat and straddled the bike. The wind was mad now, and the leaves of the trees swished together wildly, the sound louder than all others.

The bike's engine roared to life, and Dan held the helmet atop his head before putting it on. "I am not giving up, Rain! I will come back for you."

With that, he put on his helmet and spun the bike around. The rear tires kicked up grass and dirt, the clumps shooting into the air before dropping back down to the ground. He hit the accelerator hard and peeled out of the clearing.

Rain heaved a sigh of relief and squinted into the trees, hoping to see Henry. She stayed on the porch for a little while, finally lowering the shotgun though still holding it tight in her hand.

Tree branches continued to sway in the wind, but soon the rustling became less turbulent. Henry either hadn't been there or wasn't coming into the clearing, so she turned around and went back inside.

Her head swirled, and she ran into the kitchen and vomited into the sink. She wiped her mouth and tried to drink some water.

Had Dan or his friends really killed a wolf? That alone wasn't hard to believe. Humans killed wolves and vice versa all the time. But what if they'd killed Henry, her Henry? She now feared he wouldn't come back, and her punishment for trying to seek happiness would be to hang her head in shame, while Dan led her away from this cabin.

When she got inside, she noticed that the fire had died down. A couple of trips to the shed gave her enough wood to last through the night. She struggled carrying firewood and a shotgun at the same time, but it had to be done this way. She didn't dare let go of the weapon.

After gathering enough firewood to last

through the night and into tomorrow, Rain secured the back door, then double-checked the front door and all the windows. The cabin windows probably couldn't keep anyone out if they wanted to get in badly enough, but she still felt safer inside.

She stood for a long time, peeking out the curtains, hoping to spot a tuft of blonde fur running toward the cabin. Funny how only last month she'd wished the wolf would never come here again, and now here she was hoping to catch even a glimpse of him.

Confronted with only the black of night, she gave up again and wrapped herself in a blanket, digging her bottom into the corner of the sofa. Hoping she could fall asleep here, Rain had no desire to move from the safety of her blanket. She carefully placed the shotgun, loaded with silver shells, on the floor next to the sofa within arm's reach.

But how could she sleep? What a day it had been. Her boyfriend: a wolf, her ex: a stalker. Could things get any worse?

Hoping to distract herself, she tried to remember how she'd gotten to this point. It started way before she'd met Henry.

When a plague ripped through the world, it killed a great number of the population. Following the initial deaths, protests and riots rose to an all-time high. Average citizens and law enforcement officers started killing each other in the streets. The riots led to even more deaths, and that's when the looting began. It became everyone for themselves.

The world population dropped by billions in less than a decade. After ten years of a dwindling population and countries trying to maintain normal functioning, manufacturing and production finally ceased.

Then the wolves made themselves known, glad to be the new apex predator. Humans started to group together when they learned they'd have to fight a common enemy.

After the death of her loved ones and her subsequent separation from Dan, Rain found solace among a new group of people with similar interests, alcohol being one of them.

Liquor remained in solid supply both during the height of the crisis and after. No disease stopped people from enjoying the taste of alcohol chugged or shot down their throats in small glasses.

So these days everywhere Henry and Rain went, they found bottles of alcohol either one or two on shelves or hoarded in abandoned houses. Recently, Henry had replenished the supply of clear alcohol like vodka to use as a disinfectant, depleted after treating Rain's injuries when she first arrived.

On certain food runs, Rain began to pocket

other kinds of booze which led to her now possessing a small stash of various kinds of liquor. When Henry had asked, she lied to him saying they were for cooking. While she *had* been using some of the liquor for cooking, she'd also been known to take covert sips of it to help her sleep from time to time. She hated lying to Henry this way, but she'd learned some heavy stuff lately, and self-medicating with liquor seemed to be helping. At least that's what she told herself.

Maybe he could smell it on her. If so, he'd never said anything. In addition to the large bottles of alcohol standing sentry as cooking booze, she'd hidden small travel sized bottles around the cabin. Silly because Henry probably knew the ins and outs of this cabin better than her, yet she'd done it anyway.

Rain dug into the couch cushions until her fingers landed on a small bottle buried there. Amaretto, already on her lips, was perfect because she didn't need to mix it with anything. Now she could definitely stay camped out on the sofa.

Consuming the rest of the bottle happened faster than she would have liked, and she winced a little as it burned her throat on the way down. She felt a rush of warmth as it traveled to her stomach, and she sunk deeper into the sofa practically melting into it, her hands clutching the small, empty bottle.

10 Three Bean Salad in a Snap

NOISES WHICH SOUNDED like a drunk man fumbling around on the porch brought Rain tiptoeing to the door, trying not to make too much noise.

Once there she wrapped her fingers around the shotgun and crouched down to open the door hoping that if something were to attack her, they'd not expect to see someone hunched over in the doorframe.

Inching the door open, she saw not what she expected: Henry's face level with hers, not wearing a scrap of clothing, and streaked with dried blood and scratches. Rain gasped and flung the door open as wide as it would go. She called his name over and over again, wrapping him in her arms, rocked by his appearance. She couldn't see where one scratch began and the next one ended.

Scooping him up gently into her arms, she helped him walk to the bathroom and climb into the tub. She then disappeared to set several large pots of water to boil on the stove. While they were boiling, she filled the tub with frigid water from the well. Henry didn't move at all as the icy water splashed his bare skin.

Running back to the pots on the fire, she found them almost overflowing with popping boils, so she hauled them to the tub to create a more tolerable temperature. This back and forth seemed to go on forever until water lapped his knees.

When she returned to the bathroom for the last time, she saw Henry slumped over the edge of the tub with his face pointed downward and drooping between his arms, hanging lifeless in front of him.

She took a soapy washcloth to his body, remembering the first time he'd disappeared. The circumstances were so similar except now he'd not only returned with bruises but also scratches and deep gouges, and the thought that Dan or one of his friends had done this to Henry made her stomach churn. After the bath, she helped Henry slide into bed, folding the covers over him. She tried to pad out of there softly so he could rest and recover.

Dinner that evening consisted of a haphazard three bean salad of white beans, chickpeas, and kidney beans that Rain drenched with a quick herb dressing she'd whipped up. It wasn't knock-out delicious or even the most glamorous meal, but it was the best she could do. She left a bowl in the bedroom for Henry and then returned to the kitchen to eat in silence.

When she finished eating, Rain settled into the sofa holding a book with palm trees on the cover. After some time she heard Henry pacing around the bedroom.

Realizing he now hovered in front of her, she set her book aside but made sure she spoke first. "What happened to you this time?"

"I don't want to discuss it."

She balked at his response and fired back harsher than she'd intended. "Well, what do you want to *discuss*?"

"This could go very badly, and I don't want that."

"What do you mean?"

"I'm worried that I might kill you." His words came out in a whisper.

"You haven't killed me so far." She had tried to make a joke of the situation, but her words seemed to cut into him, so she reached out and took his hand. "I trust you, H."

"Having you in my life has made my existence here better, and our friendship is something that I value. I don't want to lose that." He put a careful precise emphasis on the last six words.

"I feel the same way. So what's the problem?"

"It seems my being a wolf makes things unnecessarily complicated."

She hadn't wanted to hear that, so she breathed out her next words. "How do we fix this?"

"I don't know yet."

The next night Rain found Henry reclining on the comfortable sofa across from the firepit outside behind the cabin. She shimmied into a cushy chair across from him. Her eyes caught his through the orange blaze, and he gazed back at her, an uncomfortable silence weaving its way through the flames.

At last he spoke, his voice laced with worry. "I didn't know that I'd like you so much, Rain. I am in a lonely place in my life, in need of a good friend. I think you came along at just the right moment. I have probably been more kind and more driven to build a relationship because of that. And I'm attracted to you, so I almost certainly flirt more than I might otherwise, and am more open where I might otherwise be guarded."

"Okay I get it, but unless you push me away, which I'm not going to let happen . . . " She paused for a moment, making sure her determination registered with him. "I'll always be your friend, H."

"Our friendship matters more than anything

to me. If me being a wolf ruins that, well I don't want that."

"I mean obviously, I don't want that either."

"Would it be simpler, more preferable, to just walk away right now? That's a genuine question rather than a definitive suggestion."

"I don't know what I want but it's definitely not that," she said.

"I don't know where we're going yet either. This is a traumatic, turbulent time, and I'm infatuated with you, even as I know you're important to me, and I want you in my life."

"Wow." She could only force out this single word.

"My approach has been to feel my feelings and take things one step at a time."

"I love that approach," she said, unable to breathe. "You . . . you took my breath away."

"I honestly don't think we can do otherwise."

"I know that I can't," she said. "I need you and all of your feelings."

"I've done a good job learning how to suppress my feelings, so it feels good to practice feeling them all. Keeping them down hasn't worked for me."

"I won't tell you what to do, but I will tell you there is never a need to suppress your feelings with me. I thrive where there is emotion. Die where there is none."

"I think I was dying anytime I tried not to feel." He puffed out a hint of sadness.

"Come be alive with me." She moved to the sofa and pulled him into her arms.

Time passed, the silent ticking of an invisible clock.

"I'm sorry I scared you," he said.

"No, you didn't scare me, but I didn't want to imagine not having you around."

"You're not getting rid of me."

"I wouldn't even want to try. I know you haven't been in my life long, but it feels like you've always been here," she said.

"Yeah, it feels right."

"I've also been thinking the same. Everything with you just feels right. When you asked me what I want, I think this is the best answer: I want whatever you can give me now, now meaning the present not now meaning right now."

"Then it's yours," he said.

So it was decided. Things would carry on as they had. Neither would suppress the growing attraction she hoped they'd just expressed nor would they ignore the pull dragging them into each other's arms.

They remained locked in embrace while the half moon traveled through the night sky, the clouds drifting in front of it from time to time.

"I need to sleep," he said after what seemed

like ages. "Will you sleep with me? I mean in the same bed."

She could feel a warmth building under her cheeks. "Of course, H. I would love nothing more."

Little did she know this would be a standing invitation. Every night when he went to sleep from now on, the pull to join him in his bed felt like a magnet drawn to metal. Like tonight, his strong hand closed around hers, and he led her out of the light of the moon and into the shadows of the bedroom.

11 Candy

Dusk loomed as Rain watched the sun creep lower and lower toward the horizon. Henry's frustration grew more visible as each new house they entered proved to be empty.

She glanced around, thinking every shadow one of Dan's guys. "H, we really should go."

"Let's stay a little longer. We're still okay." He opened more cabinets that stood barren.

"It's gonna be dark soon."

"I'll know if anything dangerous gets close."

"I want to go." She could feel her heart thundering in her chest.

"I don't. You take a break over there." He handed her the shotgun and pointed to a dusty chair on the other side of the kitchen. "I'll be done in a few minutes."

She let out an audible scoff, kicking debris on

her way to the chair. Henry was being ridiculous, but she'd given up trying to reason with him. This house had been emptied by someone else long ago. Just a waste of time.

When they got back to the cabin, right before sunset, an uneasiness bubbled in Rain's gut as they climbed the stairs. Something felt off.

The chaos inside hit them as soon as Henry opened the door. Books had been flung from the shelves. Rain found silverware, plates, and pots from the kitchen drawers and cabinets scattered all over the floor, some chipped, some shattered. Henry darted toward the bedroom.

"Almost all the shells are gone," he said, spitting out curses after tossing a box with two shells onto the kitchen counter.

"The ones from the bedroom?"

Henry furrowed his brow, and his tone took on a hint of annoyance. "Yes."

"But not the silver shells," Rain produced the shells that he'd hidden in the cubby under the sink, not a single one missing. "Who did this? What were they looking for?"

"I don't know."

Guilt settled on Rain because she probably could have answered both her own questions. One guess would have her blaming Dan or his men for this. They must have been looking for a wolf, but in the process they'd robbed Henry and Rain of their ammo as well as their food supply.

She lingered in the empty pantry, afraid of the repercussions that came with telling Henry about Dan. If he or his people had done this, it made them assholes, but she didn't want them dead.

"I'm scared," she whispered.

Henry pulled her body to his, encircling his arms tight around her. The drumming in her chest slowed.

He breathed his response into her hair. "It's going to be okay."

When Henry pulled away from her, his eyes burned into her, and the next thing she knew his mouth was on hers, hungry. She melted into his kiss, a kiss she'd been wanting for what felt like forever.

Time passed like drifting through a dream, until they lay shrouded by the darkest part of night with legs intertwined, her head on his chest listening to his heartbeat. His arms wound tight around her, their breathing fell into sync, and their clothes sat in a bunch on the floor.

Not long ago, Henry and Rain had been strangers, neither knowing of the other's existence. And now such a large world appeared quite small as if they were the only two who existed.

Their bodies were sticky from sweat, but the wide-open windows blew air in from outside sending them tingly chills. Rain nuzzled deeper into Henry's warmth. His whole body radiated heat under normal circumstances, but today had been far from normal.

Any time she hovered too close to him, hugged him, or shared a bed with him she could feel heat pulsating off his body. Yet now they were not as close as they had ever been, no that had happened moments ago, but she was still near enough to him to be swallowed by the steam coming off his skin. Her fingers crawled up to his hair, and she laced them through the golden strands and began to pull gently through.

"You keep doing that." He breathed a tiny moan. "And I'll want you again."

"What's the problem?" She did not stop playing with his hair.

Every previous point of contact, the hugs, the soft gentle willful touches, everything had led to this. Rain's mind traveled back to that moment. The split second before it happened, his eyes like a blue flame burned into her soul as if to say, "I know you, and I know what you want."

After that first kiss, their hands found each other's bodies, tearing at the feeble barrier of clothing, the only thing which had kept their skin from touching. She breathed heavily, matching his own, but he stopped a moment to look at her.

"You're beautiful," he said.

Her breath caught in her throat, and she

couldn't say anything for what seemed like an eternity.

"Kiss me," she said in a whisper.

Henry moved without hesitation as if jolted to obey, and his lips devoured hers once again. From then on they were caught in each other's net, unable to untangle themselves.

Her mind lost back there, her breaths became sharp, so she took a moment to steady her breathing. Henry never took his hands off her body while resting his head on her stomach. He had always been a point of comfort for her like a weighted blanket, but even more so now. As she calmed, her breaths became even, less shallow.

She laced her fingers in his hair again, pulling through the strands which felt softer than her own. She never wanted to stop touching his hair, and his face screamed silent bliss.

"I love your hair," she said, her fingers combing through silken wisps.

"I love you touching my hair," he said, and she could feel his heart beat faster every time she touched his head.

Every time Rain tried to say something, the words got caught in her throat, and she couldn't force them out.

"We don't always need to talk," he said, reading her mind.

She nodded into him wondering how he always managed to do that. How he always managed to fish out her desires, knowing exactly what she needed. Was it a preternatural gift or something forged by the time they had spent together? She had no answer to this, but she kind of hoped it was a little bit of both.

After some time had passed, neither expressed a desire to move. With his long arms Henry reached into a drawer in the bedside table and pulled out two disks wrapped in gleaming foil. He offered one to Rain and with a crinkle of the wrapper popped the other into his mouth. The cold air from outside might have forced them to stay pressed together in warmth infinitely with their legs entwined.

"Are you happy?" Henry asked.

"Blissful," she said. "You?"

"Bliss is a good word for it. I appreciate your facility with words."

"I know my way around language. This is so perfect. I just want to live in moments like these."

"'Living in a moment' sounds right."

"I never wished I could stop time more than today," she said.

"This moment is really nice. I could live in a moment like this."

"Me too."

They chatted in a dreamlike way until exhaustion settled in and sleep dragged them away with a gentle paw. Rain drifted in and out of dreams. In times when consciousness plagued her, she thought she wanted to be in his arms as much as she could to make up for so much lost time. The hours, days, and weeks she had spent not in his embrace made her feel like something had been missing from her life for a long time.

This feeling now, where she could reach over and his arms would encircle her effortlessly, was as she had said: bliss. The world could end right here, right now, and she would die happy. When she snapped back to reality, she didn't want to die yet. She wanted more of this: everything that had happened that night on an endless loop with varying interesting new things thrown in.

When Rain awoke for good, she was in his arms again. She didn't know how long he'd been up, the eternal morning person, but instead of leaving her cold and alone in bed, he held her until she had opened her eyes.

"Good morning," he said.

"It is now," she said, smiling and getting one back from him in return.

"Are you hungry?"

"Not for food."

"Me either," he said

"Oh, what do you want to eat?"

"You."

Her fingers brushed his nipples, the slightest of touches before his mouth moved on hers yet again. Neither one seemed to care that breakfast would be a little late this morning.

12 Pasta e Fagioli

MORNING MEANT CLEANING up the mess Rain had assumed Dan had made of her life. Petty. Had he been searching for evidence of a wolf? Or had he just wanted Rain to be miserable because she refused to leave with him?

While they worked at putting their life back together, Henry's face also looked fraught with worry. Neither one of them made an effort to talk, and instead let the sounds of cleaning fill the silence.

Later, contentment settled on her when she picked some vegetables from the garden which had exploded overnight, abundant with a rain-bow-colored harvest.

After cleaning, Henry had popped out quickly to see if he could find some food, and when he returned with canned beans, tomatoes, tomato sauce, and a bag of pasta, it felt like Christmas. Plus, they still had the garden teeming with vegetables.

Cooking always gave order whenever chaos crashed in her life. With the garlic and onion now fragrant, she sautéed a carrot and a celery stalk into them over the firepit outside. Once the vegetables were tender, she added Henry's canned bounty to the pot. Heaps of dried herbs and salt and pepper joined them.

When it became a bubbling cauldron, she added the tiny tubular pasta making sure it cooked until al dente. The afternoon sun warmed her as she cooked, and when they ate, a feeling of comfort washed over their faces.

That night, with full bellies and order restored to the cabin, Rain rested her head on a pillow on one end of the sofa while on the other end, Henry plucked the strings of his guitar. He said he'd been thinking about playing a song Rain would like and strummed the guitar as if letting his fingers search for some melody.

"How long have you been like this?" Rain asked.

"A guitar player?"

"A wolf." Rain frowned, trying to bring a bit of seriousness back into the room.

"I was born this way," Henry said. "I remember being a normal child. I was never a wolfchild. It wasn't until I hit puberty that I changed for the first time."

"Were you scared?"

"Terrified," he said. "I didn't know what was happening to me, but I knew that I couldn't tell my parents or anyone else about it."

Henry played a few blues or jazz-like notes. Rain couldn't be sure.

"How did you handle it?"

"Not well at first. Sneaking out a lot during the full moon. Finding out the full moon is actually three days long. I also eventually found out that the more-powerful female wolves, can change at will, which would have been convenient when I was working 9 to 5. And I was always very horny. I had what I imagine was a normal teenager libido times a thousand. After a while, I had someone to help me with my new life, such as it was."

"Shit," Rain said under her breath. "But you know I like how horny you are now."

"Really?" Henry asked, his voice marked with a hint of surprise.

"Totally. It's a huge turn on."

A mischievous smile pulled at the corners of Rain's mouth. She had a high sex drive in general, and at one point in her life she'd propositioned younger men because she thought they had the stamina to keep up with her. Sometimes they did.

Sometimes they didn't. More often than not she found them better looking than guys her own age.

Stumbling upon Henry had been incredibly fortuitous. She'd met her match, someone who could finally keep up with her but also sometimes exhausted her, the opposite of many experiences she had prior to meeting him.

He returned her smile with one equally laced with desire, but didn't stop playing. Rain closed her eyes and listened to the soft melody fill the room. The tune started to take shape, and Rain recognized it after a few notes.

"I know this song," she said.

"Do you like it?"

"I do." Rain tried to remember some lyrics and began to softly sing along.

"Do you like to sing?" Henry asked.

"I love to sing, but I don't think I'm very good at it," she said with a laugh.

"It doesn't matter. What matters is that you enjoy it."

"I find there are very few things left to enjoy these days," Rain said with a hint of sadness.

"What kinds of things did you enjoy before all this?" Henry gestured out the window as if indicating the state of the world.

"Oh, so many things," she said. "I liked going to live shows, listening to my friends' bands play. I liked riding my bicycle. Sometimes, I'd dance at clubs and drink with my friends. Mostly, I liked simple things like going to restaurants and coffee shops, shopping. Some things I enjoyed before I can still do now like being lazy, cooking, reading, and gardening, thanks to you. How about you? What do you miss?"

"I miss running water. Going to movie theaters. The thought of never being able to go to a movie again makes me sad. Phones for communication purposes. Not necessarily the internet or smartphones or computers."

"I miss those things too, but I do miss the internet. However, I'm lucky I met you. You make things infinitely less terrible. It's easy to forget that the world sucks when I look at you."

"Same," Henry said, smiling.

He played for a little while, and the air filled with music. Rain fixed her eyes on him the whole time. She had always had a "thing" for musicians ever since high school when she used to follow local bands around. They didn't have to be big famous musicians; Rain admired talent.

Since she felt she possessed no musical talent of her own, those who did impressed her. As her attraction to Henry continually blossomed without wilting, his musical skills added one more layer of attractiveness. Not that he needed it.

She already couldn't keep her hands off him and wished she could stop thinking about him naked all the time. It didn't make for productive times that's for sure. Not that anyone had much of anything to do these days. Nonetheless, they couldn't spend every waking hour using sheets as their only covering. Or could they? Rain felt her cheeks flush. Everything about Henry made her so hot all the time.

Henry broke her train of thought. "You smell nice."

"You . . . you smelled me?" Rain bristled a little at the silliness of her question, remembering he was not just a human but also an animal.

"Smell is important to me. It's less that I went trying to sniff you, and more that I just noticed," he said.

"Really? What do I smell like?"

"You smell like the soap we use, but there's also your own scent under that."

"I wonder what my scent smells like to others. People always seemed to like smelling my hair in the times before these. I used a rather expensive hairspray."

"I'll try to articulate it at some point. Usually, I don't get past associating a smell with a person and deciding if I like it," he said.

"So what does that mean in regards to me? Just that you like my smell?"

"Yes. I can still smell you on me."

"How is it?" she asked.

"Very nice."

"What does it remind you of?"

"My face buried in your neck."

"Oh god," Rain said, her breath caught in her throat. "What are you thinking about now?"

Henry looked at her intently but didn't take his fingers off the strings. "Oh, I was thinking about being in bed with you. Making out and flashes of sexy images. My face buried in your neck, your fingers in my hair and mine in yours, our legs entwined, your hands touching me."

"That was immensely more poetic than I expected," Rain said.

"Is that good?"

"If you know anything about me, you already know the answer to that."

"Yeah," he said. "Just confirming."

The sounds of the guitar drifted around her head. She was hard pressed to find a time when she didn't find Henry attractive. At first she had been captivated by physical characteristics like his shining hair that brushed the top of his shoulders and his beautiful eyes.

Over time her attraction grew into a love of his kindness, his gentleness, his unrelenting care and concern for her mental and physical well being. She was endeared to him by his constant touch. He held her hand, nuzzled her, or enfolded her in most amazing hugs. She began to crave these things, happy to meet someone in this turbulent world so tender and so loving to someone still a stranger in so many ways.

Still staring at him, a piece of her hair fell over her face. She found it and tucked it behind her ear.

"This is nice," Rain said.

"It is," he agreed. "Peaceful."

"Definitely."

Henry continued noodling on the guitar. The next song Rain didn't recognize, but its undertone rang of a blues piece. She closed her eyes again, feeling the vibrations of the warbling in her heart. She was overcome with a sudden surprising sadness.

"I don't know this one," she said. "But it's pretty powerful."

"I like this guy. I mean liked, I guess. Dunno what happened to him." He played a few more chords. "Before all this I hadn't touched a guitar in almost a year. It was a thing I kept going back to but never consistently practiced."

"I think you're pretty good now. I imagine you've had lots of time to practice these days."

"Yep." He continued playing.

She closed her eyes again, losing herself in the song. "That was beautiful."

"Your face is beautiful."

"Stop it." Her cheeks were hot, and she smiled widely. "But really don't."

"Okay, I won't," he said, setting the guitar aside and leaning in close to her. "I like you close to me, and I enjoy talking about everything."

"I can be closer," she said, inching toward him.

He put the tips of his fingers on her shirt, his shirt. While she often pulled pieces of clothing from the houses they tossed, she preferred wearing his worn, soft tees.

His tongue moved across his lips. "I like you in my clothes."

"I bet you'd like me out of them too."

A low growl vibrated in his throat, sounding almost like a purr. Rain moved her hand to Henry's waist, and he sighed softly. He reciprocated by nuzzling his forehead into hers like a cat might do. She wrapped her other hand around the side of his neck and moved it up into his hair.

"I like when you do that," he said.

"I know," she said. "That's why I'm doing it."

He rumbled a slightly louder growl before his lips met hers.

13 Dad's Easy Vegetable Soup

A SCREAM that could have shattered glass ripped through the morning air. Rain was on her knees, tears streaming down her cheeks amid a sea of green that looked like it had been hacked away by a machete.

"What's wrong?" Henry called from the doorway before eschewing the steps and jumping to the ground.

She held up lettuce leaves, robbed of their lifeblood hanging limp from her hand but could only choke out two words. "The garden."

Standing behind her now, his eyes moved from Rain, who looked up at him with fresh tears, to the disaster on the ground in front of her. Like red fireworks tomatoes lay exploded on the ground as if someone had stepped on them. The tops of all the vegetables had been sliced off as she gestured to the shriveled leaves around her.

"I loved this garden." Her tears wouldn't stop. "Why? Why would someone do this? We're gonna die."

Henry dropped to his knees next to her and pulled her toward him. She still gripped the leaves in her fists as she sobbed into his chest.

He combed his fingers through her hair. "We're not going to die."

"We don't have ammo." Her voice cracked, her tears blurring the catastrophe around her, but making it no less real. "Now we don't have food."

He let go of her for a moment and thrust his fingers deep into the earth, extracting a potato. Confusion washed over her until she realized what he showed her. Whoever had done this, was a garden idiot. Sure, the lettuces, tomatoes, broccoli, cauliflower, and cabbage were shredded beyond salvaging, but the root vegetables remained intact.

Rain wiped her face on her sleeve, joining Henry in harvesting onions, carrots, potatoes, and garlic. Rain ran back inside for a wicker basket, and they stacked the vegetables high. While it wasn't how she'd hoped to harvest the garden, the thought, that death by starvation no longer loomed on the horizon, made her feel somewhat better.

While harvesting, Rain found the roots of the

destroyed plants to be unharmed. Because nights had already grown much colder, it would be too late in the season to regrow the vegetables, but they could work to preserve them for next spring.

The sun now gleaming high in the sky, Henry and Rain worked in the garden to protect the roots before winter hit with its heavy snow making it impossible to grow anything. Whenever he'd went scavenging without her, Rain requested Henry look for a manual or a push mower to make mulch, so they could safeguard the plants in winter. She knew how to grow things as well as protect them, which was more than she could say for whoever had killed a bunch of their vegetables. He remembered her request and returned with a push mower one day.

Rain snipped down the what remained of the plants while Henry walked around the edge of the forest gathering leaves, grass cuttings, and twigs and small branches. He returned to the garden every so often to heap what he'd collected into a pile not too far away from the plants. They took turns operating the push mower, shredding the leaves and twigs to make mulch. Once finished, Rain placed it on top of the leftover roots to insulate them from the frost that would come soon even though the snow wouldn't be coming until much later.

With the garden sorted, they moved onto their next task: chopping firewood to start the winter. At first, Rain assisted by seasoning the logs Henry chopped, and when he ran out of breath, they switched tasks.

They used the small shed flush against the cabin for general outdoor storage like the push mower, shovel, and other garden tools. Rain moved those aside and stacked up the wood they chopped. Winter would be cold, and today's small stacks would get them started until they had to brave the snow to chop some more.

Chopping, seasoning, and storing firewood took a considerable amount of time, and when they finished, both of them were exhausted and covered in sweat and dirt. Cleanliness beckoned them, but first they had to boil several pots of water. Mixed with cold well water in the tub, they could create the perfect temperature. The long tedious process went a little quicker by boiling many large pots over both the fireplace and the firepit outside. They took turns filling the tub which they then covered, trapping in the heat.

Rather than sit in a tub overflowing with their filth, Henry and Rain always opted to clean their bodies in the shower corner of the bathroom. When they were filthy, it worked better as a two person system taking three things: a large bucket of well water, a bar of soap, and a considerable amount of courage.

The next step was to stand in the shower

corner of the bathroom. Rain suggested Henry should go first, but he argued if he got any dirt in the tub it would run the risk of causing an infection in her they didn't have medicine to cure. She agreed.

Rain stripped her grimy clothes off her body and held a bar of soap in one hand; her other hand naturally formed a ball. Henry poured a little cold well water over the bar of soap which Rain then worked into a lather as fast as her hands could. Next, he drenched her with a little less than half of the well water while she whimpered like a lost puppy. It was like taking a cold shower, a miserable experience. After sufficient whining but disguised in suds, Henry used the rest of the well water to rinse her off. After that she could soak in the warm tub for however long as she pleased.

As a courtesy, she didn't let the water go cold. While she was in the bath, Henry had put another couple pots of water over the fire to boil, ensuring he could soak in a comfortable temperature.

The ice shower was never a fun experience though in warmer weather it could be refreshing. In autumn it was awful, and Rain imagined in winter it would be unbearable. She understood why Henry missed running water so much. She did too, never more than during these showers. Missed it so much.

While Henry soaked in the tub, Rain busied herself chopping vegetables to make a soup. It was a simple soup using a few ingredients: a can of tomatoes, carrots, onions, and potatoes. She plopped equal sized pieces of the veggies into a pot of water, boiling with dried herbs and heavily seasoned with pepper for a bit of spice.

Her dad had made this soup throughout her childhood. When she was younger, he'd spent a few years working as a chef, and during that time Rain's family ate like kings. That aside, this soup was easy to make with the limited ingredients they had left.

While the soup bubbled hot, she snuck sips of wine from a bottle she had pulled out. It stood open on the counter next to the soup deceptively made to look like she'd been using it for cooking.

Henry emerged from the bath looking like he'd followed the aroma of Rain's soup wafting through the cabin.

"What's that smell?" he asked.

"Soup," she said.

"It smells delicious."

"Thanks. My dad's recipe. I hope you'll like it."

"I'm sure I will," he said.

"Wanna try it?" She pulled a steaming spoon of broth and vegetables from the soup.

"Obviously."

She blew on it, cooling it enough to feed it to

him. He made little delighted noises, and it brought her joy to know even after all that had happened the past week, she could still make delicious things.

"Good?" she asked, even though she already knew the answer due to sampling it moments before he came out.

"Definitely," he said.

"I'm glad."

They didn't talk much during dinner, exhausted from the day's work, the air still heavy with the loss of ammo, supplies, and now their garden.

After they finished eating, Henry cleared the table and washed the dishes. While both of them loathed washing dishes, because Rain had made dinner, Henry was obligated due to the unspoken rule of the kitchen: "I cook. You clean." He soaped up the few dishes, and Rain lounged on the sofa, flipping through a book she had no desire to actually read while the tinkling of dishes and silverware filled the air.

14 Fried Potatoes

ANOTHER FULL MOON. Another night of Henry disappearing into the woods and leaving Rain cold in bed.

Henry almost never used the heavy blanket, and she rarely used it when they shared the bed, but she was glad for it now, wrapping it around her like a caterpillar before becoming a butterfly. The chill in the air couldn't touch her as she listened for wolf noises outside, and when she heard none, she fell back asleep.

After dragging herself out of bed in the morning and frying up a potato for breakfast, with nothing else to do Rain decided she would busy herself with mundane household chores. The sheets and towels definitely needed washing as did their clothes dirtied from all the outside work. Eager to distract herself, she boiled pots of water over the fire. Most times the tub sat empty, so they often used it for washing clothes.

Though there were no demands on her time, Rain had no desire to use a washboard. Not like Henry had one anyway. When necessary, she used a small brush to easily remove most stains from clothing, thankful she didn't have to scrub everything they owned.

Boiling water, laundry soap, and the sheets went into the tub. She agitated it with a broom handle a little bit and then let it sit in there until it cooled. The rinsing took much longer and several hauls of cold well-water to get the soap out of everything.

Smaller clothes were generally easier to wash, but the sheets and towels took ages. Fortunately, Henry had more than one set of these which could be swapped out while waiting for the recently washed ones to dry outside on a clothesline.

She had to laugh at herself, washing bed sheets in a tub. When coupled with her hobbies of cooking and sewing, her life looked very domestic these days. She hadn't meant to be living as a 1950s housewife, never wanting that kind of life for herself at all.

Though Dan would have wanted her to quit her job and be a full-time mom, Rain had always intended to go back to work. Whatever her path might have been then, she wouldn't have been caught dead fetching anyone's slippers. Not then. Not now. Not ever.

While the linens were in the tub, she made the bed with new sheets and tried to read a little bit. She stared at the words on the page until they began to blur together. The book was science fiction, Rain's favorite. She loved reading about space travel and advancements in technology, things she now knew she'd never see in her lifetime.

She'd hoped one day to see that sci-fi level of space travel, and maybe even visit distant planets and moons herself. Those had always been the movies she loved the most, when the heroes fired up a spaceship to fight evil throughout the galaxies.

As she thought about not living to see anymore amazing innovations in technology, she wondered if she and Henry had ever talked about age but couldn't remember them ever having that discussion. Sometimes, she thought they were close in age, but the last time she remembered celebrating a birthday, it was not a young one, so she thought she must be older than him.

Rain guessed it didn't matter to Henry because he'd never once brought it up. Things like this hardly mattered in times of survival. She felt she did well in the age department, and for Henry, the wolf must have played a role in the way he aged. Strength and vigor seemed to seep out of his pores, plus she'd witnessed him heal overnight.

Winter threatened the air with the nights beginning to get longer and colder. Rain wondered if they'd see snow soon. Were weather conditions harsher and more unpredictable? Or was it simply that no news reports came blaring through a television to warn people of storms?

She didn't want to worry about food, but she couldn't help it, afraid what little they managed to salvage from the garden wouldn't be enough to last the winter. She wanted Henry back, so they could go out together and look for more canned foods.

More than that she wanted Henry returned to her, unharmed and alone. He'd come back injured twice, and although he'd recovered soon after, she still feared something might happen to him out there. Plus, Dan and his cronies were still causing havoc in the world somewhere. She realized she'd been staring at the same page of her book this entire time, her mind elsewhere. She tossed it on the table with a heavy sigh.

She always missed Henry during his absences, his gentle touches, his sweet nudges, his intimate caresses. She missed the way the weight of the world lifted when he laid his hands on her. Thinking about this was bound to put her in a mood, so she pushed these thoughts out of her head. She understood why he needed to be away.

Of course, she understood. While it was difficult for her, she most certainly did not want the wolf here.

The next night Rain had been trying to read the same science fiction book when she heard a loud crash at the edge of the forest. She jumped to her feet, shotgun in hand. Upon flinging the door open, her eyes couldn't find any movement. But as she scanned the area, she noticed a large tree had fallen, no doubt the cause of the boom she'd heard.

She turned around to go back inside when she heard growls and snarls. Henry came into view first, but not alone. He wrestled with another smaller wolf, though both were still quite large compared to wild wolves.

The second wolf's coloring was a deep black with flecks of tawny and a tiny bit of gray in the muzzle, resembling an Alexander Archipelago wolf. The black wolf snapped at Henry, and Rain could see patches of his fur colored crimson. He shouldered the black haired wolf off of him, but it recovered quickly, bounding back toward him, teeth bared.

Tackling soon gave way to nuzzling, licking, and gentle biting. The wolves whipped their tails in the other's snout. Though she'd only heard Henry talk about her, Rain knew without a doubt who it was. Siobhan. Henry's former partner, the woman and wolf he'd returned to many times before he met Rain. The wolf who wanted him to mate with her.

Siobhan entranced Henry. His eyes were fixated on the other wolf, not even aware of Rain's existence. The shock of what happened next caused Rain to stumble backward a couple steps. Henry mounted the female wolf. Siobhan jerked her head behind her, and her eyes bore hard into Rain. She swore she saw the wolf smile at her. Large tears rolled down Rain's cheeks, and her hands shook.

Frozen, eyes wide on the scene in front of her, Rain tried to go over her options, tossing them around in her head. She could fire a shot into the air thus wasting one of the few precious remaining silver shells. Staring at them in abject horror, she realized that she only had one option as she couldn't fire directly at Siobhan without hitting Henry. It tore her insides apart to watch Henry do this, even though they were both wolves. Though her heart ripped in two, Rain didn't want to kill him.

Siobhan's eyes met Rain's again, and the wolf snapped at Henry, pushing him off her. Head high Siobhan trotted away from Henry, but he quickly followed her and climbed on her from behind once more. He moved like a creature who possessed one goal.

Like before, Siobhan snapped her head back to Rain, and once again shoved Henry off of her.

He came bounding back toward her and mounted her again. Through this sick dance, Rain saw Siobhan demonstrate more than once who really owned Henry's affections. Rain's breath came out shaky, and she swallowed a lump in her throat.

The wolves remained locked together for a long time after their motions stopped. They twisted around, and it looked like they were trying to break apart, but they remained knotted together.

After a long time of being stuck together, the wolves calmed and finally were able to disentangle themselves. Rain tried to command her feet to walk to the edge of the porch, to meet the steps, but she couldn't.

Before Henry could move away from Siobhan, she back-kicked him hard, sending him soaring into a tree. The force knocked him unconscious. Following that Siobhan howled, and five other wolves, who Rain hadn't noticed before, emerged from the trees.

Their gray fur, mottled with streaks of black and white, resembled Northwestern wolves. They came near her, sniffed her, and then each one of them nuzzled her. The last wolf to do so was an enormous black, gray, and white beast, much larger than Siobhan and even Henry.

Rain blinked through tears, and when she opened her eyes again, one of the female pack members had shifted back into a human. Stunned for a brief moment, Rain recalled Henry mentioning female wolves could do this. The woman was significantly smaller compared to her wolf form and even though her mid-length hair flowed with streaks of gray and black like her fur, her face had a youthful appearance.

The woman brushed a clump of hair from her face, and then walked to the unconscious Henry. She bent down close enough to kiss his face but instead stroked his muzzle with the softest of touches.

Rain watched the whole strange scene with eyes wide, tears streaking down her face in rivers. She wouldn't have believed Henry would have done any of what had transpired had she not seen it with her own eyes.

Henry had told her that Siobhan held power over him, but she honestly had not believed it to be as strong as what she had witnessed. He'd been completely blind to Rain's presence, only seeing Siobhan. An interloper, an intruder like Rain did not exist in the world of Henry and Siobhan. Foolishness plagued Rain.

A few months, maybe seven or eight, blinked rapidly by, nothing compared to the years upon years Henry and Siobhan had spent together. Wolves, even these, had long been believed to mate for life. Henry and Siobhan had been part-ners long before Rain had injured herself outside of the cabin, before Henry had ever touched Rain. Rain felt like she didn't belong here, and if she didn't belong with Henry, where did she belong? With Dan?

Once again she'd been slapped across the face with the realization that happiness wasn't even a stop on her journey, much less a destination where she could live her life in contentment. She felt stupid and foolish and her stomach threatened to expel what little she'd eaten today.

Rain's tears continued to fall, drying up as soon as they hit the porch. Her eyes remained fixed on this unknown woman as she buried her fingers in the unconscious Henry's fur. Though this sight punched Rain in the gut, she couldn't take her eyes off the woman and wolves in front of her.

15 Spiked Hot Chocolate

THE UNNAMED FEMALE WOLF, still in human form, curled her hand, digging her nails into Henry's scruff. Rain tried not to gape at the woman's super-human strength as she dragged him away from the tree with a sort of roughness that showed no affection.

The other wolves, including Siobhan, remained in wolf form. Only this woman stood away from the pack as the others next moved to form a protective circle around Siobhan. They growled and snarled in Rain's direction, streams of saliva dripping from razor-sharp teeth.

Even though the woman was much smaller than Henry, she seemed to tower over him, and her gray and black hair a stark contrast to Henry's blonde fur. She tightened her grip on Henry, her claw-like nails gouging his skin so hard blood started to pool.

"I thought you would realize," she hissed, "that every time Henry left, he came back to us. He belongs to Siobhan and is a permanent member of her pack. And given what you have just seen, you should now know that you mean nothing to him. What Siobhan and Henry have is something that you could never dream of duplicating in the whisper of time that you have spent with him. We will be taking him back with us. Were he conscious, I doubt he would protest very much."

"Why did he keep returning to me then . . . if he wanted to be with Siobhan so badly?" Rain stammered.

"Temporary blindness? Temporary insanity? Who knows? Whatever the case may be, you cannot have him."

"Maybe he doesn't want what she has to offer him anymore. Why don't you let him decide?"

A wicked smile spread across the woman's face. "He appears to be incapacitated."

"Then we wait. Wait till he wakes up. And we ask him." Rain's words tumbled out in a panic.

"You are not really in a position to be negotiating with me. It appears I have . . . ," she said, looking down at Henry in her hand, " . . . the upper hand."

"You certainly have a way with words." Rain rolled her eyes.

What sounded like a chuckle resounded from the pack surrounding Siobhan.

"We are done here." The woman's punctuated her words with a sense of unequivocal finality, and she started to drag the still-unconscious Henry away.

Snarls from the pack reverberated through the trees, and they parted, making a path for the woman and Henry. The woman hoisted Henry up and sprawled him over her shoulders like a fur coat, their size difference almost comical.

In human form she was tiny, but seeing her strength in action terrified Rain. From what Henry had said, female wolves were more powerful, but seeing her demonstrate it like this was eye-opening.

Rain wrestled with her emotions, her obvious love for Henry and her pure distress and outrage for what she had witnessed. She longed for the days of peace when she and Henry wrapped themselves around each other as if nothing in the world could ever bring them pain.

Now this plague of wolves threatened everything Rain had built with Henry. With him she had forgotten how unhappy the world had made her. When they finally came together, and he nightly set her ablaze with his fire, nothing before mattered.

"Now or never," Rain mumbled.

Siobhan and her pack didn't look to be moving at any great speed, but they were still growing farther away by the moment.

With her hands around the shotgun, Rain shouted, "Wait!"

The woman stopped and turned slowly around with a smirk on her face. The other wolves turned too, but they remained positioned around Siobhan, keeping her protected.

"Drop him!" Rain's voice trembled, but anger wove through her words.

The woman tightened her grip on Henry, still draped over her shoulders and took a deep breath before exhaling it in laughter.

"I hope your shells are loaded with silver." Her eyes remained fixed on the shotgun, her eyebrows raised.

"Let's find out." Even though Rain already knew the answer, she raised the shotgun, aiming the barrel straight at one of the wolves' chests.

She squeezed the trigger. Failing to beat the timing of the shot, the wolf tried to move away but couldn't do so in time, and the pellets exploded in its shoulder. The wolf yelped in pain and doubled over. It started to shake violently and shortly thereafter began foaming at the mouth, which gave way to retching and vomiting. With the silver pellets lodged firmly into its body, the wolf took several choked breaths with its tongue out before it ceased breathing altogether. Once dead, the wolf shifted back into human form.

The man on the ground now, who greatly resembled the wolf he'd previously been, looked sweet and harmless. His shoulder was bloody, and he was quite young, maybe early twenties. His hair matched his fur and fell long past his chest in soft gray with black and white streaks.

"Hmm . . . ," Rain said, emotionless. "Looks like they are."

The woman still held Henry, and her mouth became taut, eyes narrow.

Her words came out in a furious growl. "Markus was my favorite, and we had planned to leave the pack together. Little bunny, you have two choices here: cease this immediately or this whole pack comes at you. While you could probably get one more shot off and potentially take out another one of us, I doubt you could reload before one of us rips your throat right out of your neck. Trust me, I would be first in line for that. Your call. I'll wait."

Meanwhile, another female wolf shifted back into her human form. She bent down and picked up Markus's body, draping it around her shoulders like the first woman had done with Henry.

Rain considered, actually considered, but she knew this awful woman was right. Her shoulders drooped. She probably *could* take out another wolf, but between that and reloading, one of the others would be tearing her apart before she could get another shot off. She lowered the shotgun and then her head and put one hand up to indicate surrender.

"Good choice." The woman's voice was stern like someone chastising a child.

Without setting Henry down, the woman approached the female who held Markus and reached up to stroke his cheek a couple times.

Seemingly disinterested in everything that had happened, Siobhan turned and walked deeper into the forest; the other wolves followed. They disappeared among the trees, leaving Rain alone yet again. She slumped down onto the porch, releasing everything in big gulping tears. It was incredibly turbulent loving Henry, and seeing Siobhan in the flesh and how Henry had reacted to her caused the turmoil to intensify.

She finally got a hold of herself. Even with a broken heart, she knew it wasn't smart to be sitting on the porch crying in the midst of the full moon. She dragged herself back inside, locking the door behind her. Once her breaths came out more measured, she tossed a metal tea kettle, already full of water, in the midst of the fire. She couldn't bear to eat anything, but readied herself to get stupid drunk.

The kettle whistled, shattering the nighttime silence. With shaking hands, she dumped the single package of hot cocoa mix from the pantry into a mug that said *Eat a Dick* in beautiful cursive script. She whispered her thanks into the air that whoever had ransacked the cabin had been kind enough to leave the one package of sweetness to kill the bitter that plagued her.

The chocolate powder bubbled as she poured boiling water over it. Then she dumped a considerable amount of Irish whiskey, from her hidden stash, into the mug. She grabbed the blanket on the sofa and pulled it up to her neck. The spiked cocoa scalded her tongue, but she didn't care much at all.

16 Shots

RAIN STAYED near the window all day. It felt like someone had been smashing cymbals over her head, and more than once she ended up bent over the kitchen sink dry heaving. Having eaten very little, nothing came up except the occasional tang of acid.

She'd killed wolves before. Now she wondered whether killing one who hadn't been directly threatening her or what Henry had done made her feel more sick. She reckoned it was probably both.

She didn't want to do anything. She didn't touch the gramophone, had no desire to prepare a meal, and couldn't even think of trying to read. Her insides twisted into knots.

Before she had known Henry's truth, she worried during more than one of his now infamous disappearances he would never return, but this time the thought consumed her. It threatened to swallow her whole.

Siobhan and Henry's connection was all-too apparent now. As he had recounted to Rain, he'd never left Siobhan. Liberating himself from her had only been a recent development in their long history, and even though he'd pulled himself from her for a time, he had confessed to Rain he'd never been able to sever ties to Siobhan completely.

She shuddered. The power Siobhan had over Henry, made live right in front of Rain, was uncanny. Witnessing it with her own eyes, now made it real. Maybe it was time to face facts. Henry belonged to Siobhan as that horrible woman had said. Rain had no desire to possess Henry the way Siobhan had; she simply wanted him to be happy and free to make his own choices.

Not being a wolf, nor ever having had a partnership like theirs, Rain admitted to herself she didn't fully understand their relationship. Had Siobhan's unhealthy desire to control Henry pushed him to distance himself from Siobhan? Maybe he wanted to experience life as an individual rather than as someone whose whole identity had been wrapped up in his relationship with Siobhan.

Whatever the case may be, Siobhan was stronger than Rain in more ways than one. She exhibited an emotional control Rain couldn't match. Her physical strength was superior to Rain's and as the pack leader, Siobhan held a commanding power over her wolves.

A thought came over Rain. What right did she have to continue to inhabit this cabin? It belonged to Henry. At first she'd been a guest here, recovering so she could meet up with Dan, but that had never happened. Why? Because Henry had shown her pleasures she'd never even dreamt of? No. It was more than that. She'd fallen in love with him, but relief came over her when she realized she'd never expressed those feelings. After watching Henry's behavior with Siobhan, he didn't seem to love Rain at all. He'd forgotten about her. Typical.

Her time here had expired. She grabbed a backpack and shoved her few belongings into it. A couple of pink and black shirts and sweaters, some underwear and cargo pants. She'd often lounged around the cabin in Henry's soft tees, and realizing she had one on now, tossed it on the bed in exchange for one of her own. She set the bag next to the front door where the shotgun leaned against the wall. She'd take that too, as well as her one coat which hung on a hook by the door.

Fuck that asshole Dan for leaving her hungry. When she left Henry this time, she'd go back to the lodge, beg Seoyun and her other friends to take her back. If she had never left, none of this would have ever happened. Supposing that they wouldn't take her back, she'd travel the wide world alone. Maybe that was her destiny after all.

No more crying. No matter how much pain she felt. In truth, she felt numb. The shock of everything she'd seen still burned behind her eyes, and she kept playing it on a loop. For some reason her idiot brain decided to focus on the part that hurt the most and repeat it over and over: Siobhan pushing Henry off of her, and Henry intoxicated, returning to mount her again and again. Her hands went into her hair, and she clawed at her head.

"Stop . . . stop . . . stop!" Her voice shattered the icy silence.

She didn't want to think about this. She didn't want this memory. Yet at this moment she found it hard to recall any other memories of Henry. It seemed like all the happy, peaceful times had been overwritten by a scent-drunk Henry mounting Siobhan over and over again until he gave her what she wanted, the potential for cubs.

In the kitchen plagued with these thoughts, Rain found herself staring at the tiny bottles she'd hidden around the house now dotting the kitchen counter like some kind of weird alcohol museum. She started pouring and draining glass after glass of liquor until buzzing, and full-blown inebriation was on the horizon.

Her next move shocked even her as she let out a primal scream. Rain hurled the glass against the wall where it shattered into a million tiny pieces, some of which sprung back at her, leaving small cuts on her arms. She collapsed onto the floor in tears. So much for not crying.

Rain loved Henry, probably not in the same way Siobhan did, but her feelings for him were no less significant. Henry cared about her, but the fear that maybe he didn't love her suddenly overcame her. It seemed foolish of her to worry about his feelings. He valued honesty and cared for her in the purest way, but sometimes she felt his true feelings were a mystery.

It was feasible he had feelings both Siobhan and Rain at the same time but in different ways. Rain didn't want to think about this either. Her life with Henry had been very "la vie en rose." Did knowing it now make her wish it were different? Maybe. Maybe not. Rose-colored glasses were only a bad thing if removed. But she'd not chosen to take them off; they'd been ripped from her. No choice. She wanted it back, the idiomatic "pink life."

She wanted those days where she and Henry sat with their arms around each other, and no one else in the world existed. Those days were gone. Once the universe unearthed something of this magnitude, it couldn't be buried in the ground again. It would remain in view for all eternity.

Staring at the wall she had thrown the glass at, Rain spaced out and began to pile glass shards. Her fingers colored with tiny ruby pinpricks, but she felt nothing. No physical pain anyway.

She sunk farther down to the floor until her eyes were level with the hill of broken glass, an arm's length away. She imagined herself as a miniature figure attempting to climb this glass mountain. Tiny Rain took a few steps upward before tumbling down to the ground and ending up in a pool of blood each time. This horrible vision dragged her to sleep.

Agony rippled through her body when she awoke. Her fingers burned from all the little lacerations now darkened with dried blood. Her body ached from the way she had fallen asleep, face down on the kitchen floor. Darkness shrouded the cabin in the ebony of the deepest hour of night. When her eyes adjusted, she began to clean up the broken glass again. She couldn't even think about where to put it, so she set it on the kitchen counter.

A voice cut through the silence, Henry's voice. "Rain."

Heart pounding, she almost fell backward upon hearing it. "Fuck."

When she finally looked across the room, she saw a head of blonde hair hunched over in the corner. Henry gazed up at her, bruised and beaten and his eyes colored with defeat and distress.

"Rain," he said again. "I'm so sorry. For every-thing, for hurting you."

The understatement of the decade. She didn't respond, only stared at him for a long time. She tried many times to say something, but the words kept getting stuck in her throat, and she choked back tears. Finally, she couldn't hold back the torrent any longer, and tears carved paths of anguish down her face. She coughed through the sobbing but yet still couldn't say anything.

She thought maybe perhaps she didn't have the words to express this level of hurt as she'd never been hurt like this before. When he finally stood up, his nudity stood out more than before, but instead of being aroused as she might normally be, she found it irritating. She walked away, grabbed a pair of sweatpants from the bedroom, and tossed them at his face.

"Why are you here?" Her voice dripped with cold annoyance.

"Where else should I be?"

"With her." She hadn't meant them to but the words came out in squeaks.

"I want to be here with you." His voice was cool, unwavering.

She wanted to believe this, but right now she wanted so many things that could never be. Most of all she wanted a time machine to travel back into the past, and she had so many different ideas of how she could use said device.

"I was worried about you."

Rain scoffed. "Why were you worried about *me?*"

"Because I care about you, and I hurt your feelings."

She started to seethe. "I think 'hurt my feelings' is a bit of an understatement."

"Fair enough."

"Maybe you don't understand the scope. Because you're being ridiculously casual about this."

"I'm hoping by talking with you I can better understand the scope, but if you're looking for someone to scream or sob, that's not me."

"No, I'm not looking for that, but the words you're saying indicate that it's not that big of a deal when in actuality it's a big fucking deal." Her tone was caustic.

"It's a very big deal to me. I want to understand what you're feeling and what you want going forward, and I want you to understand me more."

"Okay, but I'm gonna need you to stop acting like I just caught feelings, and you had nothing to do with that because it's really starting to piss me off."

"I don't mean to make it seem that way,

because you're right, it's not. This is about us sharing our feelings, mine included." His voice remained even.

"You've not shared much of your feelings with me. In fact, unlike me you're very good at shutting off your feelings."

"I'm good at it, but I don't think it's good for me. 'Shutting off' might not be the right way to describe it. Maybe 'repress until they explode.'"

"Yeah, well, forgive me, but that's stupid, and it hurts me more because it makes me feel like you don't fucking care, whether that's true or not."

"I know. That's true for everyone in my life I've ever cared about. I don't want to keep doing it, and I am working on it if that means anything."

"Well, I'm glad to know I'm not the only one who's treated like this, I guess." Rain couldn't keep her thoughts off Siobhan, the last place she wanted them to be.

"It's a thing everyone who's close to me finds. I'm shuttered about my emotions all the time even when it's not productive to be. I can sound like a robot often."

"Well, I thought I was different and privy to a side of you not everyone sees."

"You are. The fact that we're having this conversation is proof."

"I guess." She breathed out an exhausted breath. "I still feel like shit."

"Me too. But I'm still here, and I won't run away."

"Well, that's completely different from, like, everyone else who has ever been a part of my life."

"They suck. I'm here for the hard part too," he said softly.

"Yeah, well this is the fucking hardest thing for us yet in my opinion."

"I think so too," he said. "But it makes me happy you're still here."

"I don't know how to do this, H, and that's the honest truth."

"I don't know how either, but I'm trying to communicate because that is the best idea I have. The only thing we can do is try and take one step at a time."

"I feel like my heart's been ripped out." Her eyes filled with tears.

He held out his hand to her, but she stared at it for what seemed like ages. Inside it felt like being split in two. She wanted so badly to hate him, to be angry at him, but at the same time she also wanted to reach out and grab his hand and pull him into an embrace. Because she didn't know what to do, she simply stared at his outstretched hand. She hoped she didn't feel this kind of harrowing duality forever.

"I'm here because I want to be here with you," he said.

"I only ever want to be with you. I don't want to be without you. I need your touch."

"I'm not going anywhere unless it's a full moon." His tone had become more lighthearted.

It didn't have the intended effect, and she started to cry again. His face twisted.

"I'm sorry," he said. "I meant it as a joke."

"I know," she said, finally putting her hand into his.

"I love you." He said the words like he'd said this to her every day since they'd met.

And she thought, maybe he had loved her all along. "I love you, too."

He closed his hand around hers, and with one fluid movement pulled her body into his, catching her and securing her in his arms. She wept into his chest. He held her, rubbing her back affectionately.

There was no way to measure the length of time they spent in this embrace. Yet, neither one prepared to move away from the other. She didn't know if it helped or if it even fixed anything at all, an air of relief settled about the room. Turning her head, she wiped her tears on her sleeve, but didn't move from his arms.

17 Quail Eggs

FTER SOME TIME Henry tenderly pushed her away from him, and looked with slight alarm at her hands and arms, cut up from the glass.

"You're hurt," he said, not as a question but rather a statement of fact.

Rain kept a comment regarding the emotional hurt to herself as she nodded to the broken glass piled on the counter.

"Ah," he said. "Stay here."

He disappeared, returning shortly thereafter with a small damp towel. He lifted her onto the kitchen counter, away from the broken glass and cleaned her hands and arms. He then poured a small amount of clear alcohol on the towel to disinfect her wounds before bandaging her up, mirroring the day they met. Soon the ivory towel was tinged pink.

"This reminds me of the day I showed up here. You took good care of me."

"I'll do my best to always take care of you," he said. "But you never told me what happened to you."

Rain blew out a breath. "I generally gravitated to people who made me feel safe, and the last group I was with was no different. They were a bunch of cool badasses. They brought a real 'fuck the world' attitude to the table. It was great for a while. People paired up, or some had throuples or polyamorous units. I occasionally hooked up with whoever would go down on me, but relationship-wise, I never really tied myself to any one person or group.

"In addition to the sex, we drank a lot, sometimes until we passed out or threw up. We drag-raced whatever vehicles we could find that still had gas in them. Sometimes we played chicken and crashed the cars into each other. If we were extra bored, some good old fashioned destruction of property via a baseball bat would do. It probably wasn't a smart way to go about things, but it was fun and helped us pass the time in between full moons."

"Wow."

Rain continued, "The fact that we behaved irresponsibly from time to time perhaps led us to drop our guard, and our numbers began to dwindle. Before I met you, some wolves had killed off three of our people, and I was actually on my way to meet a friend when I stumbled upon your cabin.

"On my way through the forest, I found a quail's nest buried under a clump of grass full of eggs with no mother nearby. I carefully took them out of the nest, and put them in a little pouch I had. When I got up from the ground, my foot got caught in a tree root, and I rolled it going down. The eggs got smashed, and I just laid there forever in so much pain, hoping to just hurry up and die. It got darker, and the darker it got, the more scared I became. I fell several times and totally lost my way trying to navigate the forest while injured. I guessed maybe I wasn't going the same direction I had come from and thought I heard a wolf out there.

"When I reached the clearing, I must have ended up a long way from where I'd started because I'd never seen this area before. When I heard a guitar, I thought I should chance asking whoever was inside for help. And well you know the rest of the story. You saved my life that night, H. I don't think I could ever repay you. Who knows what would have happened to me if I had stayed out any later."

"It was nothing. I just wanted to make sure you hadn't been bitten by a wolf. I think that would have made us enemies." He ended with some uneasy laughter.

"Would it? You told me about your history, wolves like you who were born that way. I know there are others too, ones who become wolves via bites. Ones like you are enemies with those who become wolves when they're bitten?"

"We call them Shortcut Wolves. Wolves like Siobhan and I were born wolves. The product of mating. A breeding female couples with breeding males, and she increases her pack numbers with cubs. The most successful breeders are the mother and father of the pack. I don't know who the originals of our kind are. I don't think any wolves know."

"Oh." Rain didn't quite know what to say.

"Like all animals, over time we evolved. We became stronger, faster, but the female wolves have always been the most powerful among us. Some renegade wolves found they could turn humans into wolves after a bite, a transfer of the venom in our saliva to their blood. It transmits kind of like a virus. They were able to create more wolves through this shortcut. Shortcut Wolves."

"I never thought I'd find the history of wolves so interesting," Rain said.

"People like Siobhan are quite traditional and don't associate with Shortcut Wolves, and I didn't want to associate with anyone, which is why I came to this cabin."

"But you associated with me."

"I did," he said.

"And you never kicked me out even after I'd healed. I kinda always wondered why."

"I came to like you very quickly. So many things about you. Your voice, your ease at talking to me, a complete stranger. You made me feel comfortable, like someone I wanted to open up to, to share things with."

"Oh." Her cheeks burned with heat. "I feel the same way about you. When we met, I felt a very pressing warmth from you which I hadn't felt in a while, and to be honest I wasn't sure what I should do with it. I knew that I wanted to be, at least metaphorically if nothing else, wrapped in that warmth. I always felt calm and comfortable with you, and my life was so fucking turbulent that I needed that calm. There was also, despite being constantly surrounded by so many people all the time, an aching loneliness that seemed to creep into every part of my life."

"I noticed too that we had that loneliness in common, so I pushed harder to know you, which might account for the pressing warmth. I entirely agree that I feel reassured and calmed by your presence, and I wanted that to continue. Being 'wrapped in it' is good wording. It always felt safe. I had been seeking that peacefulness for a long time, years, and recently the turbulence in my life had kicked into overdrive, so I decided that if I could provide some to you and myself at the same time, I would."

"Well then, I'm glad you pushed so hard," she said with a half-smile.

"I always wanted to be near you. I like physical contact with people I feel safe around, like you. At the time I got the sense that you liked it too, so I hoped at the very least we could have that easy physical connection."

"It did seem easy, didn't it?"

"So easy," he said.

"But then, I didn't anticipate falling in love with you, and more than that I didn't expect the avalanche that followed after that. Nonetheless, I still feel pulled to you."

"Yeah, I agree. I feel it too. You're an interesting and kind person, and I want to be near you. I am insanely attracted to you sexually, obviously, and I really need the affection you offer me. I wish I had been honest about so many things from the beginning, about what I am, about Siobhan. I guess I was scared."

"My heart is a little sore. That hurts more than anything else."

"Well, that I want less than anything else. I never want to hurt you."

"Until last night, you never had. You always made me feel amazing. I always felt like there wasn't anyone else on the planet whenever we were together."

"There really wasn't during those times."

"No one's ever made me feel that way, honestly," she said, her voice colored with sadness and years of damage done.

"Wow. That's terrible because you deserve it."

"I don't think I deserve any of the happiness life has ever given me, but I honestly feel I deserve all the sadness," she said.

"Rain, you deserve happiness." Henry looked at her then like no one else existed in the world.

Her hands and arms cleaned up and bandaged, he pulled her into his arms once again.

"I love you, Rain."

"I love you, too, H."

She needed his embrace right now, but she also needed the time to recover from this recent heartbreak. A stormy life constantly upended by the trials and tribulations that came with knowing and loving Henry.

"What happens now?" she asked.

"In regards to what?"

"Siobhan mostly." She pushed the words out with effort.

"She'll remain in wolf form for about two months to gestate her pups."

She noticed he referred to them as "her" pups and not his or theirs. Rain wondered if she had the strength to discuss it further. She decided she needed to.

"*Her* pups?" she asked.

Henry sighed. "They could be mine or they could be another's. As pack leader, Siobhan is also the breeding female of our pack, but she has bred with subdominant males before. While I have been with her for close to a lifetime, there's no rule that says she needs to be with me exclusively, especially sexually. Over the years she has bonded with different males to increase our pack, notably when I refused to mate with her. So while some people previously believed that wolves mate for life, this isn't always the case. Females have ultimate control of the pack, and Siobhan's goal, as the breeding female, is and always has been maintaining her pack. She will do this by any means necessary even if that means tempting the animal in me into fucking her while she's ovulating. I can guarantee, though, that I was not the only one she fucked this cycle."

Henry didn't swear much, but when he did it this time, the words came out as if he felt disgusted by his behavior. Still, a twinge of pain filled Rain as she recalled Henry being bewitched by Siobhan. She believed Henry when he said he didn't want Siobhan, but she also knew he was part animal. Animals operated on instinct like when Henry had been instinctively drawn to mate with Siobhan, when she chose him as one of her mates and intoxicated him with hormones.

He had demonstrated a complete lack of power and control around Siobhan.

When she thought about it deeply, she could see no version of her life without Henry in it. Nor did she want to live to see such a life. The only thing Rain could do now was trust that Henry honestly wanted to be with her. But how many times would he return to Siobhan in the future? She had no answer for that and believed even Henry couldn't respond to such a worry.

She focused on his eyes for a long time and for once in her life, she didn't know what to say or how to fix this. A long time passed before she spoke again.

"I killed one of the pack. I'm not sorry about it." Even though Rain did not consider Henry her enemy, the other wolves still were, especially Siobhan.

"They will probably come for you, but trust me that I will do everything I can to keep them away from here." He wrapped his arms around her.

Rain's heart still ached, but warmth and comfort enveloped her body, and she felt safe.

18 Fiery Black Beans

IN THE MORNING the whole cabin exuded warmth when Rain stepped out of the bedroom looking for Henry, rubbing sleep from her eyes. He sat on the sofa reading a book, and when he saw her emerge from the bedroom, he rushed to embrace her.

"Good morning," he said.

"It is now."

He hugged her tighter, and she smiled into his chest. She brushed some of his hair away from his shoulder and burrowed her face in his neck. She breathed in his scent, and he did the same.

"You smell good," he said.

"What do I smell like?" she asked.

"Like candy, sometimes coconut, and *you*."

She smiled and remained in his arms, unmoving. "I love you."

"I love you, too," he said.

She pulled away from him to look at his face. His beard had grown in a little. She rubbed her hand across the light sandpaper landscape.

"Looking rugged this morning," she said. "I like it."

He reddened a little. "You do? I've never been called rugged before."

"I do," she said, kissing both his scratchy cheeks and then his lips.

"I get really bad with shaving. I don't like having facial hair, but I don't like shaving either."

"As someone who's done an awful lot of shaving in her life, I totally get it."

Over the next couple days some normalcy returned to their lives once again. Rain couldn't say if her heart had even begun to mend, but she suspected it had not. She felt a kind of haze surrounding her those first few days like walking through a dream. Things didn't seem quite real or palpable.

She didn't know how to voice her feelings to Henry, so she tried to communicate via touch. She hugged him a lot, and reached out to touch him even more. His chest, his waist, his hands. Rain didn't know if this was the right course of action, if this only provided temporary relief, or if it was the path to fixing what had been broken. Yet, she needed to feel that he was real, physically in front of her.

Then whatever warmth had been sucked out

of her life by the events of the past few days slowly began to return little by little. It felt like the sun rising over the trees, setting the grasses in the clearing ablaze. He always ignited in her a kind of passion she feared had long since died out, lost to apathy and the litany of the mundane, the sameness, the unpredictability, an eternal plague.

When Henry came into her life, her old life began to smolder, reduced to a heap of ashes indiscernible. She rose into her new life with him like a phoenix from these ashes, and whether true or not, he always made her feel as if he viewed her like this, as a beautiful and mythical creature. These days she always had his attention, and she didn't know how she'd achieved this nor did she feel like she deserved it.

Henry seemed to be treading softly during this time. He didn't request any sort of physical touch from her. He simply reciprocated her affections. His arms took her in, his hand held hers when she offered it, his body yielded to her grasp.

Once in a while he'd ask if she needed a hug. She never said no, answering like there was nowhere else she wanted to be than in his arms. One time while there, tears welled up in her eyes and wet his shirt.

"Are you okay?" he asked.

It seemed like ages until she could force the words out. "I don't think I'm okay, H."

"What do you need?" he asked.

"I don't know." She realized it was the truth as she said it.

She didn't know how to erase what she had seen from her memory. A memory burned into her brain like a brand she never wanted.

"I'm here," he said. "And I'm not going anywhere."

She paused before saying, "I just need you to love me mercilessly today."

"Loving mercilessly is one of my talents."

He strengthened his hold on her then. She breathed out the smallest of sighs. She told herself she had to trust this truth, but the difficulties in trusting what he said came not from not trusting him. Rather they came from past trauma. From years of lovers pledging their undying affections and then disappearing into the mist never to be heard from again or from lovers who'd left her for someone else.

Tears hung in her eyes, glassy but refusing to fall. She wanted an eternity with Henry, but she had trouble believing it feasible.

After that emotionally fraught evening, both Henry and Rain wanted to stay in bed longer than usual. When they finally did decide to get up, it was well past lunch time.

"Are you hungry?" he asked.

"Yeah, you?"

"A little," he said.

And she remembered that she rarely caught him in times of intense hunger.

When he returned the other night after being with Siobhan, Henry said he brought a bounty of food back to mitigate the destruction done by whoever had ransacked the cabin and destroyed the garden.

Now he unloaded from his pack several cans of beans, vegetables, and tomatoes, oil, a box of stale tea bags, and a couple of packages of cocoa mix. It didn't look like much, but two people with very little food supply saw a feast.

"The bread is gone, and I haven't made more yet," Rain said, thankful the raiders didn't take the remnants of the giant bag of flour. "We're running low on fresh vegetables. Let's see what we can do with what we have."

Henry set the tea kettle over the fire until it started to whisper a whistle. Rain pulled cans of corn, tomatoes, and black beans from what Henry had brought back, while he plopped a tea bag into one mug and cocoa mix into another.

The variety of spices they still had like cumin, chili powder, and cayenne would make some fiery black beans, so that's what Rain decided to mix together in a large pot over the fire. Henry stirred the beans for a while.

Rain brought bowls over, and Henry ladled the simple meal into them. She carried the tea to the table in front of the sofa, and he placed the beans there. They nestled themselves into the plush cushions, grabbing the bowls of beans.

Not a gourmet meal, but the best she could do with what they had. The fire roared comfortably now, and Rain sipped hot tea, Henry cocoa. She thought today might be a good day to make some more bread. Neither of them had any desire to go look for more food.

After lunch they stayed lounging on the sofa for a while. Rain read to Henry from *Lord of the Flies*, a book she regarded as one of her favorites. He rested his hands on various parts of her body while she read. The weight he put on her made her feel safe, secure, such a simple thing she never knew she needed until Henry had done this.

Without warning Henry reached over and embraced Rain, and she felt overwhelmed with emotion. She wanted to feel something other than all the harshness this world threw at her day after day and definitely wanted to forget about Siobhan. She could only respond in choking sobs.

"I can't get it out of my head, H. Every time I close my eyes I see you, as a wolf, fucking Siobhan."

He didn't say anything but instead pulled her body close to him, and she pressed her legs tight together in front of him. She cried into his bare chest until exhaustion overcame her and she fell asleep in his arms. She felt his hands on her, his arms holding her tight throughout the night.

In the morning Rain awoke groggy and chilled to the bone as she felt around the empty bed. The last place she remembered being was on the sofa and thought Henry must have carried her here sometime in the night. That thought brought a small smile to her face.

Rain sat up and looked around, rubbing her eyes, and almost as if on cue, Henry appeared in the doorframe holding a cup of tea for her. With some effort, eyes red and puffed with pink rings underneath, she widened her smile. He handed her the tea, and sat on the edge of the bed crossing his legs.

"Good morning," he said.

"Hi."

"I have an idea."

"Oh?"

"If you let me, I'd like to take care of you today."

Rain thought about it and then finally said, "Yeah, I think I'd like that."

"Good. Come with me."

He gently pulled her out of the bed, and she fell into his arms, so he hugged her. He held her there as long as she needed and didn't move until she decided to pull away.

When she finally did, he wrapped his hand around hers and walked her to the bathroom. He sat her down on the stool in the shower corner, asked her to get undressed, and walked out and returned with a large pot of warm water. He added soap to a small towel, and rich with foamy bubbles, began to wash her.

His movements were docile, making certain she was comfortably warm while he scrubbed her in the tenderest way. Rain squeezed her eyes shut as a wave of contentment washed over her. She had cleaned up Henry more than once, so she welcomed this reversal of roles.

Once finished, he wrapped her in a large luxurious towel, and asked her to wait. It seemed he'd been busy while she'd slept as Rain looked into the tub and dragged her hand through the cool water there. He returned several times to continue filling up the tub mixing huge pots of boiling water into it.

He then picked her up and gently placed her in the water. The water flowed over her body, warming her soul. Ease sunk into every muscle. While she sat in the tub, he sat on the stool beside her and brushed her hair until baby soft. After that, he dismissed himself, leaving her alone to relax there.

After some time when the water started to chill, Henry returned as if a timer had gone off in his brain, offering her a fresh dry towel. He led her to the bedroom, asking her sit down on the bed. A look of seriousness and longing settled in his eyes as faced her and ran his hands over her shoulders and down her arms. However, he did nothing more than trail his fingertips over the softness of her skin.

The air outside made no noise, the room still dark. Rain collapsed back onto the bed and let the pillows swallow her. Henry crawled to where Rain had become one with the bedding. He moved her body close, his arms encircling her tight. She nuzzled into his neck, his pheromones intoxicating her.

Rain's thoughts swam with Henry and how he made her feel desired, coveted. She hadn't felt this way in forever and if asked couldn't have said how long it'd been. Her whole life she'd felt unwanted, but Henry swooped in and craved her. He wanted her to be happy. He wanted to give her pleasure.

He held her for what felt like an eternity, and bliss carried her into dreams.

19 BAKED ARTICHOKES

ONE AMAZING EVENING in the care of Henry wasn't enough to mend Rain's whole heart, but it was a start. She wanted more than anything to forget about Siobhan, to forget about what she'd seen. If she never had to think about her again or that, it would be too soon.

For lunch, Rain wanted to try something new. She'd used the makeshift Dutch oven for baking bread and wondered if she could use it for actual baking.

In the morning Henry had gone out to comb the vast landscape of abandoned houses and by late afternoon brought home a couple of cans of artichoke hearts, half a package of flavorless Italian bread crumbs, a small jar of peanut butter, as well as some more staples: cans of beans, tomatoes, various other vegetables, and a bottle of lemon juice.

There were still a few root vegetables from the garden, so she set some onion and garlic to sauté with the bread crumbs over the fire. She hoped it would wake them up a bit because when she sampled them she found their flavor definitely resembled paper more than anything else.

She cut the artichoke hearts in half and placed them, plus the oil from the jar, in a small dish that would fit in the Dutch oven. Then she drizzled on some lemon juice and dumped the bread crumbs over that before adding sizzled onion and garlic on top.

Since all of the ingredients were already cooked, they simply needed to warm up together. She put the small dish in the Dutch oven and put it over the fire keeping an eye on it at first. A salad would have been a nice accompaniment as she remembered holding the shorn leaves in her hands.

She called Henry, who had had his nose buried deep in a book. He nestled a bookmark between the pages and set it down near the sofa before joining her at the kitchen table.

"This looks great." A smile spread across his lips.

"I'm glad to hear that. You know, I like making you smile," she said.

"You're good at it."

Henry put half of the artichoke dish on a plate for her and took the other half for himself. They chatted about nothing in particular.

When she reached her hand out to him, he curled his fingers around hers sending a wave of heat through her arm and into her body. She shivered with delight at the feeling and loved that Henry could always make her feel some kind of way.

"What should we do today?" His question broke her musing.

"I have no idea," she said.

"It seems the kind of day to wrap ourselves in blankets, sit in front of the fire, and just read."

She smiled. "I think I'd like that."

He took both her hands in his. "Thank you for the delicious food. It made me happy."

"That was easy," she said.

"I'm easy," he said.

"No, I just know what you want."

"It's you. I want you."

She felt her face flush, and she swore she stopped breathing for a moment. Before the mess with Siobhan, she remembered how good he'd been at taking her breath away, relieved to know he still had that effect on her.

Bowing her head and looking up at him, she recalled the whole reason she'd fallen in love with him to begin with. Not his flirtations or even the way he made her feel when their bodies were pressed against one another. She'd fallen in love with the man under the beast. The soft, kind-hearted, gentle Henry who always took care of her and wouldn't want to hurt her for anything in the world. The man who needed Rain's affections, her touch, and her love. The man who came alive whenever they were together. That was the man she loved.

She could tolerate the animal, the creature operating solely on instinct, but she definitely didn't love the wolf. Oftentimes, it helped to attribute his behavior as the wolf to a different being. That way she could put the creature, and the way he'd fucked Siobhan so wildly, in an unrelated box in her mind, lock it tightly, and throw away the key so she never had to open it ever again. Rain didn't know if this method would work, but it was her best idea yet.

Henry walked hand in hand with Rain to the sofa. The dishes, he'd said, could wait. He touched her face and asked her what kind of book she wanted to read. The fire blazed mandarin on his face. The cabin with its interior of grays and deep blues was dim, lit only by the fire and the skylight.

In the mood to read a classic, Rain pulled *The Great Gatsby* from the shelf. Even though she'd read it so many times, she never tired of the book.

Henry, on the other hand, chose *The Picture of Dorian Gray*.

They nestled into the sofa opposite one another, feet sliding under the large fluffy blanket, making sure their legs were touching. It seemed they never not wanted to touch one another. Even the smallest seemingly innocuous touch was important to both of them, but Henry had always said he thrived on physical touch.

Upon staring at Henry's book selection more seriously, she decided she'd rather hear him read *Dorian Gray* to her and asked as much of him. Henry said he thought his voice was okay, but didn't feel any particular way about it. However, he said he was happy to oblige, and she repositioned herself under his arm, which he then wrapped around her. She felt overcome with warmth and nuzzled her head into his neck. Her body curled into Henry's. She thought she might fall asleep any moment.

When he began to read, his even voice resonated throughout the main room, the words dancing off the pages. With the book in one hand, his other found his way along the curve of her body.

With great feeling of ease draped around her, her eyes started to droop. She tried for a while to keep them open, but soon gave in and passed out. Not bored, simply soothed.

It had been a while since things had felt this

comfortable with Henry. Lately, the days had been so tumultuous. Very few moments of pure peace existed either of the physical or emotional kind.

Henry stirred, his body jostling Rain slightly. She opened her eyes, stretching her arms upward. She saw the fire had gone cold, but his body heat had managed to keep her quite warm. Henry moved himself from under Rain, got up and threw some logs on the fire until it blazed again, the deep crackling sound of the logs the only noise in the cabin.

Darkness now blanketed the clearing and forest. The stillness outside mirrored the calm inside with no wind to be heard nor a single sound from the wide world.

"I think there's no place I'd rather be than here with you in front of the fire," Rain said.

Henry returned to the sofa and slid into her, wrapping his arms around her waist. "This is the best."

When the fire was roaring again, they draped the blanket over themselves once more, and Henry continued reading to Rain where he'd left off earlier. They stayed like this well into the night, reading, staying close and warm, and enjoying each other's company.

This is the version of Henry in the version of the world she liked best. In an ideal world, they could spend every day happily cuddled together, but this was no ideal world. Not by a long shot. Their world was never ideal, especially these days.

In the time she'd known Henry, the difficult times sometimes outweighed the pleasant times. The more she thought about it, however, the more she came to realize that the severity of the difficulties made them seem far greater than the quiet peaceful moments. What was life if not fraught with trouble? A life less ordinary, perhaps.

As the night wore on both Henry and Rain got sleepy again despite their earlier nap. When neither wanted to stay awake, Rain got up and taking Henry by the hand, led him into the bedroom.

While Rain stripped down to her underwear, Henry took off all his clothes. This had been the familiar nighttime routine. The conventionality reminded Rain of a time before her whole life had been uprooted by trauma.

Henry crawled into bed and held his arms open wide for Rain. She nestled herself close to his body, no longer chilly and turned her head towards his, placing a soft kiss on his lips. He reciprocated her kiss, and his lips held her there like they were locked this way, a hug for their lips. When they'd gotten enough, Henry looked at Rain, his eyes fixed on hers.

She giggled. "What?"

"Nothing," he said, moving his hands over her body. "I just love you."

"I love you, too." She embraced him tighter until sleep took them away.

20 Henry's Favorite Loaded Baked Potato Soup

HENRY SPRUNG UP, startling Rain awake. The morning sun streamed through the curtains in thin golden beams.

"I forgot," he said with as much excitement as someone like Henry could have. "I got you something."

Rain looked at him, brow furrowed, but a smile spread across her lips. "For me? A gift?"

He disappeared into the storage closet, and she heard the clatter of him rummaging around on a high shelf, one she couldn't reach. He returned with his hands behind his back, beaming at her like a child.

"Pick a hand," he said.

She chose his left which he presented to her empty. She scowled. Giving her a wicked little smile, he returned both hands behind his back but produced them again, holding an instant camera. Her gasp shattered the cool silence of the cabin.

"It still has film in it," he said.

"Do you think it still works?"

"I didn't try it. I wanted you to try it first."

Warmth spread through her. She thought he'd perhaps forgotten when she casually mentioned her love of photography. She never thought anything like this would've come of it.

She took the camera from his hands, investigating it from every angle. When was the last time she'd seen a camera, let alone an instant camera? It had to have been years for sure.

"Do you think we should take a practice shot? Then see if it develops?"

He nodded, so she held his hand in hers in front of the fireplace in a somewhat artistic posed style. She pressed the button on the camera, snapping the picture. The image shot out from the slot, and Rain took it, carefully extracting it all the way, and placed it on the table in front of them.

They waited, barely breathing. Soon the image began to appear. When it had fully developed, the colors were dull, muted, but their two hands clasped together appeared in the photo.

"This is the best gift ever!" Rain squealed. "Thank you so much, H."

"You're welcome," he said.

"Let's try another!"

She asked him to sit on the sofa and then crawled in between his legs and nestled her head into his neck. She turned the camera around, but couldn't get the distance she needed with her short arms.

Henry plucked the camera from her hands, giving her a look that said "may I?" She felt a bit reluctant to hand over the camera at first, but when she saw how he had angled it just right, her chest loosened. He took the picture, and they both waited in anticipation, eyes boring into the developing image. Their smiling faces and his blue shirt next to her pink one started to appear.

"Oh, H," she said, near tears. "I really love this!"

She picked up the photograph, overwhelmed with the sudden desire to take a hundred photos of them together. She also wanted to take pictures of every mundane thing. Every moment preserved on film.

Peering at the counter, it wasn't possible. It read there were six photos remaining. These had to be used with a certain level of discernment, so she decided to take only photos of him or of the two of them. No need to preserve the mundane. Everyday things were of little importance in this world. Henry mattered more than anything, so she would make sure she took the remaining photos with the utmost of care.

She crashed hard into Henry then, wrapping him in her arms. Maybe he didn't understand her feelings completely, but this gift meant the world to her. Losing technology had been a huge loss to the world, of course, which meant Rain as well. Certain things would probably never resurface again in their lifetime. Yet the precious little working technology that remained was often a huge blessing, especially when it represented something one of them loved like Henry's music or Rain's photography.

She held him whispering "thank you" over and over again and when she broke away, showered him with kisses.

At some point later that evening, Rain coaxed Henry off the sofa where he'd fallen asleep with a book on his lap. Upon hitting the sheets, they fell back asleep almost at once, drifting apart and then back together throughout the night.

In the morning, Rain awoke to the sound of Henry pulling open the curtains, flooding the room with sunlight.

"Good morning," he said, crawling back to her in bed.

"It is now." She smiled at him.

"Don't get up. Stay with me like this for a while."

"Oh, I wasn't planning on getting up, and I'll stay like this with you all day if you want."

"That makes me happy," he said, returning her smile.

They cuddled together for an undefined period of time until Rain suggested they should eat something. While she paced around the kitchen thinking of something to make, Henry did some indoor exercises, calisthenics like push-ups, and pull-ups in the bathroom doorway. He practiced some handstands, showing off to Rain he could do a few handstand push-ups. This did not go unnoticed.

Rain decided to make Henry's favorite food: a delicious baked potato soup. She had Henry start a fire in the fireplace and then peel some potatoes while she made a roux. She told him that it wasn't difficult to make but still important. A simple recipe calling for equal parts flour and fat. Now, of course, the best fat, as Rain knew very well, was butter. But because no one had seen butter in who knows how long, oil would have to do.

She toasted the flour in oil, and in the absence of milk used water to make some semblance of a creamy base. Into that base went the potatoes Henry had peeled and chopped followed by some minced onions. A perfect baked potato soup should be loaded with cheese, cheddar ideally. Yet she didn't want to think about how cheese had become a ghost of a food.

Rain checked the seasoning, adding some garlic powder and thyme, plus salt and pepper of course, and cooked it until the potatoes were tender. Despite the missing ingredients, Henry loved her creation. He reiterated that it was the best soup ever, thankful she had made his favorite food.

After breakfast, Henry bounded into the bedroom and collapsed onto the bed like he hadn't slept in weeks, and Rain fell in next to him. His arms encircled her as always.

He said he wanted to cuddle with her here in this bed, feel the softness of her skin on his, and remain pressed against her for as long as he could. In response, she nudged closer, moving as close to him as she could. Rain buried her face in his neck. She loved the way his hair smelled like the faint aroma of their shampoo mixed with the scent of him.

"This is nice," he said after some time.

"So nice," she said.

He ran his hands over her body once again, and she returned these affections touching him all over. He pressed his forehead gently against hers; she responded by closing her eyes and rubbing back against him.

She loved the way he touched her. Always soft and gentle, touches laced with love. The electricity of these feelings flowed through his limbs and shocked her to life, awakening all her senses making her feel more alive with Henry than she ever had. If nothing else would come from this experience at least there was that.

At the same time, Rain loved touching Henry and wanted her hands on his body and more than that she wanted his on hers. They felt like fulfilling a need or filling a glass long since emptied by the harshness the world had thrown at her.

In her long colorful history of lovers she had never known another like Henry. Determined. Selfless. Giving. Insatiable. Thinking of how he never wanted to quit pleasuring her put him miles above any other man she'd ever been with.

But that was not what this moment was about. This moment they dedicated to touch. Arms wound. Legs twined. Faces buried in necks. Simple. Pure.

"Wait," she said.

She tore herself away from him with some effort, and reached over to the table beside the bed grabbing the instant camera.

"This day is so perfect." She smiled so wide it almost hurt her face. "I want to immortalize it."

It didn't matter that their hair was a mess. It didn't matter they weren't wearing clothes, and they'd thrown a sheet over their naked bodies. It mattered that they loved each other. It mattered that their cheeks were flushed, and they were happy. That mattered the most.

Rain crawled back into Henry's arms and handed the camera to him. He snapped a picture of them as they pressed their heads together. After the photo, Henry pressed his lips to Rain's forehead like it was the most natural thing to do. She squeezed her eyes shut and absorbed his warmth through this kiss.

She put the camera back on the table and pinched the image between her fingers, huffing out her impatience while it developed. Their faces started to come into focus. As before the colors were not as bright, but the image of two people full of love stared back at them.

"I love this," she said.

"You're a good photographer," Henry said.

"Well, you took the picture."

"With your eye."

"I think I just have a good muse." She sat up, winked, put the photo on the table, and turned back to him, kneeling.

"This is definitely my idea of the perfect day," Henry said, still reclined on the bed.

"Come over here and love me properly." She smiled and pulled him up to her.

She embraced him hard and lingered in his neck before she kissed it. He breathed out a soft sigh.

"What about your perfect day?" he asked.

"My perfect day needs to have sunshine. Also, the temperature has to be perfect too. Not too hot. Not too cold. My perfect day has to have no physical pain on my part. It has to be full of delicious food. It has to begin and end with amazing sex where I'm falling asleep in someone's arms. There has to be lots of laughter and lots of touching," she said.

"I think we've covered some of those things."

"What about the rest?" she asked, raising an eyebrow.

"Well, I think I can help you with the rest."

"Specifically?"

"Amazing sex." His voice dripped with confidence.

"Oh yeah?"

"Yeah," he said, kissing her hard.

She yielded to his kiss, his mouth hungry on hers, his tongue swirling around hers. As if by instinct, her hands settled on his hips, and he let out a soft growl. He gently pinned her down on the bed and held her arms there for a brief moment. Her breathing became shallow and sharp.

Without warning he climbed off of her and slid down into the bed next to her, her back close to his front, the small spoon to his big spoon.

Henry placed his hands as if they lived on her body, like they'd become a part of her, an extension of her curves, her breasts, the small of her back, her hips, her neck, her waist. She breathed more evenly with his weight on her in this gentle way. She felt a long missing contentment and fluttered her eyes closed letting him continue to explore her body with his fingers.

21 Pumpkin Soup

THE LEAVES on the maple tree in front of the cabin looked like they'd been set on fire as they blazed, ruby-colored, into the sky. The weeks prior they'd started to fall until they covered the small yard in front of the cabin, and Henry had been saying something had to be done about these leaves littering the small yard in front of the cabin.

One chilly morning, Rain followed the sounds of raking to the front of the cabin and came out to the front porch to stare at Henry while he worked. Henry stood in front of a giant pile, moving more leaves into it with the rake.

Despite the chill, he wore short sleeves, and she could see his veiny arms ripple as he made repeated raking motions. Why was he doing this? They had no place to dispose of the leaves, though they could be used for a second layer of mulch.

"Hey, you," she called to him, smiling.

"Hey, yourself," he said, turning to her.

The pile of leaves next to him was massive now, almost as high as his waist, and shined a bright crimson color in the morning sun.

"Looks like you've been busy," she said.

"I guess so." He evaluated the scope of the work he'd done while she'd been asleep. "I enjoy raking leaves. I don't get to do it that often. It's kind of like a Zen garden, full of repetitive movements."

"Fair enough. Why are you so sexy?" She eyed him up and down as his brow glistened with sweat in the sunshine.

"Why are *you* so sexy?" He shot the response back quicker than she could have anticipated.

Not expecting such a rapid-fire response, Rain burst into a fit of giggles, looking down at herself drowsy from sleep, cozied up in sweat pants and a baggy pink sweater drooping to expose a bare shoulder.

He laughed with her. "I didn't expect that reaction."

"I didn't expect you to say that."

Rain barreled down the steps of the porch and tackled him in a hug so powerful he fell backward into the pile of leaves. They sprayed in every direction and then fluttered back down to the earth like flaming snow, shining cardinal in the morning light.

She sat atop him, and his hands moved to her waist as he pulled her body close to his. She leaned in, pressing her lips into his.

Coming up for air he said, "You know I'm going to have to rake these leaves again."

"Well, you enjoy it so . . . ," she said.

He weaved his fingers in her hair and pulled her head to his, bringing her mouth to his in a soft yet passionate kiss. The leaves ornamented themselves in his honey strands, setting his hair afire in a sea of red. He looked like a forest sprite, the scarlet crown a stark contrast to his glassy blue eyes.

As always, his body felt warm under hers, and she didn't even feel the morning chill anymore. She rolled away and crashed down into the leaves next to him, sending another scattering of leaves out in one direction.

"You keep making more work for me."

"Sorry, I guess I should go and *leaf* you to it."

She started to get up, but his long arms reached up and pulled her back into his embrace.

"Not so fast."

"What do you need?" A flirtatious smile spread across her lips.

"Just you," he said.

"It seems we need the same thing, each other."

"Agreed."

He smiled at her, pure and genuine, and she interlaced her fingers in his, kissing him again.

"Okay, you enjoy your raking."

But as she tried to get up, he pulled her back down and spun around until he hovered over her, pinning her down. "Got you."

"Whatever are you going to do with me?" She made a mock damsel-in-distress voice as a devilish grin spread across her face.

Licking her lips, she hoped for naughty things, very naughty things. Henry surprised her then by swiftly standing up and pulling her to her feet before throwing her over his shoulder.

"Henry!" She laughed, slapping his bottom. "Put me down!"

"Never." He gave a small wicked laugh.

Once back to the porch, he kicked open the front door, went directly to the bedroom, and tossed Rain onto the bed. Because she could feel her arousal building at this game, she decided to stay put.

Henry left the bedroom and returned with a rope she'd never seen before. He took one of her arms and tied it tightly to one post of the bed, replicating it with her other hand.

"Oh wow . . . okay." She breathed hard, not knowing what would happen next but eager to find out.

He surveyed his work and then got up from

the bed and left her there. When he got to the doorway, he turned the top half of his body toward her.

He looked at her with a severe seriousness. "Be a good girl."

"Henry? Henry! What the fuck? Henry! Untie me!"

He stopped again and with his voice still weighty said, "Shh . . . don't make me gag you."

Her eyes grew wide, and her words got stuck in her throat. She heard him call back to her from the front door.

"Good girl."

Rain heard raking noises from outside as it sounded like Henry had left the front door open. She struggled against the bonds holding her to the bed, swearing under her breath at making no progress on the ropes.

"This is not what I had in mind," she breathed, looking down at her body, still fully clothed. "Shit."

When the sounds from outside stopped, she heard Henry walk up the stairs and onto the porch. Her wrists red, she stopped wiggling, afraid he'd see her and chastise her again. Terror on her face, she remained still when she saw him enter the bedroom.

As soon as he saw her face, he softened and rushed to the bed to untie her. She let out her breath, which she swore she'd been holding since he'd appeared in the doorway. Henry reached out to her with the sort of caution one would use in approaching a dangerous animal.

"Henry, what the fuck?" She spat the words at him.

"I'm sorry, Rain. I had meant for that to be fun, but I wasn't thinking."

"What if it was near the full moon?" Her words were rich with anger, but her breath came in gulps. "What if you'd changed?"

"Fuck, I'm sorry."

"Furthermore, we never talked about *this*." She gestured angrily to the ropes.

"I'm sorry," he said again. "I'll be more careful with regard to everything."

She blew out an exasperated breath. Though she'd known via her makeshift calendar it wasn't time for a full moon, she wanted him to try and understand her feelings.

The animal still terrified her. Though she'd tried to accept this part of him, loving Henry and everything he was still continued to be unpredictable. Plus, next time they were in the bedroom, they'd need to discuss acceptable sexual practices.

"Do you need a hug?" A hint of apprehension lingered in his voice as if he wasn't sure of the right course of action.

Rain nodded with uneasiness. He enveloped her in his arms, and the tears came slowly at first until they were practically gushing. Tears fell onto his shirt, as he stroked her hair with a gentle touch. For a long time she held onto him until her tears finally stopped.

After that, Rain felt relieved to have some physical space from Henry when he returned to rake more leaves. She thought cooking might be a way to get her mind off Henry's idea of bringing bondage play into the bedroom without communicating it first. Whenever she closed her eyes, all Rain could see was a wolf bounding into the bedroom and shredding her to pieces, while she remained unable to break free of the ties holding her there.

Among the vegetables Henry had brought back was a can of pumpkin puree, and after a long time of just staring at the can, Rain thought she ought to try to make soup with it. Because there was no milk or cream, she'd have to make a sad soup with water, hoping the canned pumpkin could replace the missing creamy taste. Either way it would have to do.

Happy to have her mind on a situation she *could* control, she started by finely mincing some garlic and finished by slicing an onion, plating each of them separately. The simple repetitive motions of cutting up the vegetables eased her mind a bit.

She set the pan over the fire and drizzled in some oil. Once hot, she dumped in the onion rings, never taking her eyes off it as she stirred. It began to turn from white to light tan to a deep golden brown, perfectly caramelized. After that she swirled around the garlic for a brief moment because burnt garlic contributed a ruinous bitter flavor to any dish it found its way into.

One sip of white wine for her and then a swirl into the vegetables worked to deglaze the pan. Maybe she'd have two more sips. Those two sips turned into two glasses, and she'd never been more thankful she'd hidden alcohol around the house.

Her eyes were glazed as she added salt and a bevy of long-expired dried spices including thyme, basil, and oregano. Finally, she plopped in the canned pumpkin. She gave the soup a couple of whisks. The best she could do to blend every-thing was to use a rotary hand blender. Not her preferred method, but it made a fairly creamy and edible soup.

When that was done, she pulled it away from the fire slightly so it would stay warm without burning. Buzzed from the wine, she went back to the front of the cabin and told Henry that break-fast was ready.

They arranged themselves with a bit of distance from one another on the sofa in front of the firepit. Rain filled two bowls full of the steaming pumpkin soup, handing one to Henry and then taking the other for herself.

"I hope it's not terrible." Her words were distant.

"Nothing you make could ever be terrible."

He slurped up a spoonful of soup and claimed it was good, but right now she didn't care if he liked it or not.

"How was the Zen raking?" She asked, her words slurring a little.

"Zen," he said.

Rain thought she'd kill for a little bit of Zen right now.

22 ORANGES

A COUPLE OF DAYS PASSED. Like clockwork, Rain added the days to the calendar. Two and a half weeks before the full moon.

They still had a few potatoes to make some winter soups and stews. Although Henry was a wolf, he ate primarily vegetarian food like Rain did because she did most of the cooking. Henry knew how to make a few things, but said he didn't particularly enjoy cooking like Rain did.

She found a measure of comfort in the kitchen. In the past, she'd ended up there whenever life had been chaotic. Order existed amid pots and pans. Things made sense. Put an array of ingredients together, be rewarded with a tasty dish.

Since she didn't eat meat, she'd started to cook at fifteen and over the years practiced what worked and what didn't plus found out what she excelled at making. The current state of the world allowed her a lot more time to experiment with food.

Rain tried to focus on cataloging the food they had left, but her mind became tangled, still troubled by what had happened in the bedroom. She didn't know how to broach the subject with Henry. Every time she'd tried, the words wouldn't come out of her mouth, so she let it fester in her stomach like bile.

In the afternoon, Henry asked Rain if she wanted to help him pick some bright, ripe fruit from the large orange tree behind the cabin before heavy snow covered everything. She said she'd help, thinking anything would be better than having to figure out how to talk to Henry about the bondage incident.

Both of them could easily reach the oranges drooping on the lower branches, but the ones high up proved more difficult. Henry shimmied up the tree with apparent ease, much to Rain's astonishment, tossing oranges down to her. She caught them, putting them into the basket resting on her hip.

When the basket overflowed, he climbed down, pressed his lips softly to her forehead, which she leaned away from instead of into, and took the basket from her. They went back inside and added the oranges to the storage.

"Do you think there are still cows?" Rain asked, as she unloaded oranges, anything to avoid talking about being tied to the bed.

Henry's face flooded with color. "I don't know."

She looked at him, accusations written all over her face. "Wait a minute. Have you ever eaten a cow?"

He blinked at her as if thinking of how to answer delicately. "Not the *whole* cow."

Her face wrinkled in disgust, and she stuck her tongue out through a frown.

"Why did you ask about cows?"

"I was just thinking about cheese," she said, a bit embarrassed to confess how much time she actually spent thinking about cheese. "I miss cheese so much."

"Me too."

Even though both Henry and Rain knew that animals, especially wolves, ruled the planet now, she couldn't recall seeing many domesticated or farm animals which seemed strange. Easy prey? Of course, Henry had more inside knowledge into the animal population than Rain did, but he offered no further information. After that the cabin seemed to drown in silence.

For some time she felt like she'd been carrying around a backpack full of rocks: finding out the truth about Henry, wrestling with accepting him, chasing the wolf away from the cabin, watching him with Siobhan, and being shocked by his behavior a couple days ago.

Slumping on the sofa, she squeezed her eyes shut, hoping to push out the pain that lingered behind them finally losing all the weight to sleep.

Rain awoke with a strong sense of alarm to the pressure of Henry's hand on her shoulder. Her shirt soaked with sweat, she shook his hand off her body.

"Shit." She breathed out several heavy breaths. "You scared me."

"I'm sorry," he said.

Without thinking, she shrunk away from his hand as he tried to reach out for her again. She scrunched her face up, wearing this look for several beats. He took a seat at the far end of the sofa and said nothing as if waiting for her to speak first.

"Henry I . . . ," she started, but the words balled up into a lump in her throat.

He remained still, patient. Rain pulled her hands from the top of her head through her hair.

She closed her eyes hard and heaved a great sigh. "I've been scared."

"Of me?" he asked.

Though she knew he already knew the answer, she nodded.

"I know I contributed to that more than I should have by what I did the other day," he said.

"Yeah." The word came out in a whisper.

"I'm really sorry for that," he said. "I had meant for it to be sexy, fun. I wasn't thinking. I didn't think about how that might scare you coupled with the knowledge of what I really am, the wolf I mean."

"I know, H." She softened a bit. "I'm trying really hard to accept all of you. To love you despite everything, but to be honest it's fucking hard."

"I get that," he said.

"I just don't know how to deal with this. How to deal with any of this. The way the world is. The way you are. Siobhan. Everything is just . . . fucking difficult."

"I know. I don't know how to either, but I'm trying to communicate because that is the best idea I have."

"Yeah, I've always believed that communication is the most important thing."

"I want to fully understand what you're feeling. I want to make amends and keep this relationship going. Can we agree on that?"

"I can try, H." She breathed out a sigh. "It's the best I can do right now."

"The only thing we can do is try and take one step at a time."

Henry held out his hand to her in his signature, palm-up style. She remained in limbo for a long time. She wanted to touch him, to put her hand in his, but she didn't move.

After a while, she reached out to him and took his hand. He closed his eyes, responding to this with a slight squeeze of her hand.

A look of relief spread across her face, but it was impossible to mask being emotionally drained. Within their discussion, she realized she hadn't properly articulated that being tied up and left in the bedroom was the scariest part of all.

"Do you want to go to the bedroom with me? Or if you want, you can sleep here."

"Don't be ridiculous," she said. "Of course I want to sleep with you."

"Okay." He sounded relieved as he got up, and still holding her hand, he pulled her up.

"Can I give you a hug?"

She nodded and pushed her body gently into his. Despite everything, this moment reminded her how perfectly their bodies always fit together like two puzzle pieces which had been tossed out of the box and lost to time.

"I love your hugs," she said into his chest.

"Same," he agreed. "You're an amazing hugger."

When Henry enfolded her in his arms, the level of comfort she felt there was unprecedented, never feeling this kind of peace with another person.

She'd not even felt this level of ease even with Dan, the man she'd married. Her marriage had been turbulent, fraught with pain, anger, countless tears, and weekly arguments which erupted in months and later years of distress.

She couldn't help think about Dan sometimes when she was with Henry because in so many ways they were polar opposites. Two different people would undoubtedly love in different ways. But after having been with someone who showed his love via financial support, it felt rather refreshing to be with someone who showed his love through his actions and physical touch.

When she let go of his embrace, she pulled him into the bedroom. They both collapsed into bed, falling asleep soon thereafter.

Rain didn't sleep as well as she had hoped she would, waking up several times throughout the night. One time when she woke up, she found Henry staring at the ceiling. She had to talk to him and now.

"Henry?" she whispered, turning her head so she could look at him.

"Yeah?"

"I'm not okay."

"What's wrong?" He rolled his whole body toward her. She hesitated, opening her mouth and then closing it again. Finally, she resolved that keeping this to herself would only cause it to fester. Nothing would be fixed.

"What you did the other night . . . tying me to the bed . . . you . . . you never asked me if it was okay to do that, and you just left me there. It was fucking traumatizing."

He reached out to her, cupping her hand in both of his. "I'm sorry. I didn't mean to scare you. I thought it might be fun, but now I know how you feel, and it'll never happen again."

She sat with his words a moment, and he also remained still.

"What about it was scary?" he asked.

"Well, several things. First, we never talked about using bondage in the bedroom. I don't think I would've had a problem with it had we discussed it, but I was so confused when you just left me there. I didn't know why you did that or when you were coming back. I didn't know if you were gonna leave me tied up in this cabin alone or if you were gonna come back as a wolf and devour me."

"I understand. I will never tie you up and leave you alone again. And I can't speak for the wolf, but know I have no plans to devour you."

"Okay, well, I really want to believe that," she said.

"Is there anything else you need me to hear right now?" Henry asked.

She breathed out through her nose. "I think, maybe, I'm okay for now."

"If that changes, I always want to know."

She nodded and rolled into his arms, where he held her once again.

23 Spicy Two-Bean Chili

WHEN RAIN OPENED her eyes the next morning, she saw Henry gazing at her, already awake. His expression looked soft, kind, and full of contentment. He smiled slightly but made no other movements.

"Been awake long?"

"Not long," he said. "But I didn't wanna get up."

"Oh, the beauty of not having to go to work. Could you imagine if we met at a different time, in a different place?"

"I imagine it would be awful. Going to work everyday sounds exhausting," he said like he'd never worked a day in the past.

She laughed and nuzzled closer to him. "Do you think we'd be friends?"

"I would hope so."

"I'm glad I met you like this though. The world is quite scary these days, but there are no demands on our time. We can just be like this together."

"Just you and me. It's nice," he said.

"You make me feel so comfortable."

"Same."

"And I love how warm your body is. I wanna live next to your body."

"I'm happy to warm you up," he said.

A grin spread across her face. "You make me feel really good, so I don't want to let you go, like physically."

"I want to keep doing that," he said.

She loved the way he always reacted so positively to her desires. "I think about how good it feels with your arms around me, like an off-the-chart level of security."

"It does feel secure," he said.

"Like uncannily comfortable. Warm. I just feel like I'm okay," she said.

"That makes me happiest of all."

He moved his arms around her tighter, and she sighed. He always made her heart flutter, which sounded like someone with a crush. Yet her feelings for Henry ran deep like canyons and were definitely reciprocated.

"Do we have to get up?" Rain buried her face in Henry's chest.

"We really don't."

"I'm not gonna argue with the idea of staying in your arms all day."

"I'll hold you," he said.

"Please."

Rain smiled, and he returned her smile. It was so easy to forget Henry was an animal. The man now keeping her warm and cozy was so kind and gentle, so loving, so unthreatening, not like a dangerous animal at all.

She looked into his eyes, the softest blue like summer hydrangeas or forget-me-nots. Unlike any eyes she'd ever seen before, she couldn't help staring into them. They mesmerized her like a fire, which sometimes danced with cornflower flames.

Everything about him filled her with longing, his hair, his eyes, his significant eyebrows and sharp features, the way his whiskers grew in patchy. More than any physical characteristic though, his benign nature enchanted her. His deep voice was always coated with a softness.

But behind those eyes, she sensed a hint of exhaustion like someone trying hard not to be tired all the time but failing miserably. Despite looking like someone who could sleep for ages and still never be entirely awake, he always gave Rain his full energy, all his love, all his affection.

She could live a million years and still never be able to repay the kindness Henry had shown her from the moment she stumbled into his yard, an odd little injured thing. He'd been under no obligation to help her or continue to allow her to reside with him, but he'd done all that and more.

Nor was he required to care for her, care about her, develop a strong attraction to her, or even fall in love with her, but that's what had happened.

She wanted to carry the memories they'd made thus far and the feelings they evoked with her always, grip them tight and never let them go. That notion made her snuggle closer to him, and he reciprocated with equal attention.

Later, Rain decided to make chili for breakfast. She diced up onion and garlic and stirred them in a little oil in a big pot over the firepit out behind the cabin. To that she added salt and a hearty dose of chili powder and stirred them around enough to cook the seasonings until the chili powder made her nose tingle. It heated up the aromatic oils in spices which always made a dish taste better.

Glistening black beans, fat kidney beans, and a can of juicy tomatoes went into the pot all with their respective liquids adding more depth. Everything simmered until the flavors came together.

While they ate, cottony snowflakes fluttered down in a dance not unlike a ballet. The snow came lightly at first, and then gradually became heavier as Rain imagined music picking up and a stronger tempo causing a wilder frolicking of snowflakes. She stopped eating to watch the dance of white outside the window. Having not seen much snow her whole life, it always mesmerized her, looking upon it with a childlike wonder.

"It's beautiful." Her voice came out in a whisper.

"Yeah," Henry said.

"I never spent much time in snowy places, so this is kind of otherworldly to me."

"Fresh snow is my favorite because it's fluffy and crunchy and hasn't turned to ice yet."

"Cute." She smiled at his description of snow. "It certainly is beautiful."

Later, Rain's eyes started to feel heavy, and Henry had difficulty keeping his open as well. Full bellies and being blanketed in warmth tended to do that. After little deliberation, they decided a nap would be the best course of action.

Even though it was midday, the heavy curtains, they'd closed after breakfast, made the room quite dark. The fire caused shadows to dance around their faces. Henry said he felt hot and pulled off his shirt, exposing his smooth chest with only a couple of patches of hair.

Rain liked looking at his body but not as much as she enjoyed touching it. He wiggled out of his pants, and since he hadn't bothered to put on underwear, there was nothing left to remove.

Following suit, Rain took off her clothes as well, and Henry laid back pulling her into his arms. One thing Rain loved more than anything was the feeling of skin on skin. Henry's skin was particularly wonderful to be pressed against because he always radiated heat. During these colder months, she welcomed it more and more.

"Do you want to stay here?"

"The bed would definitely be more comfortable," he said.

"But more tempting."

"Tempting?" he asked, raising an eyebrow.

"I might be tempted to ask for your face between my legs."

"Oh really?" He pulled her to her feet, a smile pulling the corners of his lips. "I suppose if you do, the gentlemanly thing to do would be to grant your request."

As he walked her to the bedroom, his hand gripped hers but not too tightly. Her whole body shook, a chill rattling her, so he pulled her into his gravity, his inferno immediately swallowing her. Immersed in him, feather-light feelings of peace settled onto her body.

They dropped down into the bed together, and she weaved her legs around his like they belonged there.

When Rain rolled over, her eyes landed on the calendar. Tonight would be a full moon according to her tracking, but Henry hadn't left yet. In fact, his arms encircled her tight, and she suddenly felt like she couldn't breathe.

"Henry?" Her voice came out fraught but serious.

He made a slight noise that sounded like "hmm" but said nothing else.

"Henry." She tried again with more urgency. "It's supposed to be a full moon tonight, but you're still here."

"I'll be fine." His words came out heavy, thick with sleep.

24 Peanut Butter Toast

RAIN FELT the poking of needles on her bare skin. Still drowsy, never the morning person, she could think of no worse time for Henry to play a prank on her.

"H, stop," she mumbled, but the pinpricks continued, and she shoved him off of her, snapping her eyes open.

Claws. Clawed hands and feet. She screamed loud enough to shake the trees before shoving Henry away from her and running for the shotgun.

Henry emerged from the bedroom, shaking the sleep out of his eyes.

"Rain." Her name came out in a growl that scared even him, and he looked down at his elongating fingers in astonishment.

"Get out! Get out!" Her hands shook, one on

the door handle, the other on the shotgun. "Get out of here!"

Whipping back and forth, his eyes, now yellow, burned into her as if trying to sear her alive. She flung the front door open, and wide-eyed he looked from his hands to her one last time, before bolting through the door and leaping down the steps.

Rain didn't even check to see if he'd cleared the porch before slamming the door, trembling hands latching the locks. Her heart thundered in her chest. He'd never done this before, been so careless as to transform inside the cabin.

Tears streaming down her cheeks, she pawed into the couch cushions, uncovering no more small bottles of hidden alcohol there. She tore the cabin apart. There had to be something remaining, but her search turned up nothing.

After giving up on finding any booze, Rain made herself a cup of tea and toasted a piece of bread over the fire. She spread a thin, almost transparent sheen of peanut butter on the toast, as she didn't want to face Henry if she used the last of it.

Nibbling on the toast her mind drifted to eggs and butter, but she still missed cheese most of all. She couldn't remember the last time she'd eaten cheese and actually didn't want to think about it. Before all this, cheese had easily been her favorite food, and she frequently longed for a salty block of perfection. Thinking about food felt so much better than thinking about the fact that she'd almost died, even if she didn't have that food.

She breathed the tiniest sigh and continued chewing. Once finished, she didn't bother to wash the minimal dishes, dropping them into the sink instead.

She went back to digging around the drawers for alcohol, but instead she happened upon the drawing she'd been working on when Dan's unwelcome arrival had prevented her from finishing it, so she pulled out the art supplies, scattering them around the kitchen table with her unfinished drawing. This could distract her for a little while.

Rain sketched most of the day until she got hungry again. The shorter days and longer nights of winter made the time Henry spent as a wolf longer. For the first time since he'd run out of the cabin this morning, she looked out the window, watching the sun light up the clearing and the tops of the trees as it sank lower and lower until it slowly disappeared beyond the mountains. She fixed herself something simple to eat, a piece of bread and some beans, heated over the fire.

After she'd finished eating, she laid back on the sofa and stared at the skylight. What an awful day. She missed TV. Internet. Smartphones. All quality technology long gone now. She eyed the art supplies. Should she draw some more?

The familiar sounds of a motorbike in the distance derailed her thoughts.

"Fucking hell." Rain jumped to her feet, grabbing the shotgun on her way to the door. "And here I thought this day couldn't get any worse."

She stepped out onto the porch in time to see Dan jump off the bike and remove his helmet mirroring their previous encounter.

"I thought I told you to fuck off, Dan!" As with every past argument near the end of their marriage, her voice had already become louder than necessary.

"Please, I told you that you have got to follow me," he said. "My people and I are well-protected. You will be safe with us. It is not safe here! I assure you."

She aimed the shotgun at him. The wind shook the trees ferociously. The past two days had been beyond windy. She heard a howl resound through the forest. Leaves swirled in mini-cyclones through the trees.

"Did you trash the cabin? Steal our ammo and food?" She asked, angry tears behind her eyes.

"I will admit it. I did it to persuade you to come with me." He tried to step toward her but she shook her head "no" at him. "It is clear that you cannot survive without my help."

"You don't think you might've contributed to

not being able to survive? We could've starved to death! You asshole! And the garden?"

"Garden? I do not understand. Rain, please. We have your food and your ammo, and we can protect you. I can protect you. I will take care of you. I can take care of you because I know you better than anyone else. You cannot do it on your own or even with this other man. You need my help, like always."

Rain scoffed before breathing the calm back into her voice. "I'm going to ask you one more time to leave."

"No," he said, matching her calm tone. "I do not think I will be leaving alone."

Dan turned his back to her and riffled through a leather bag attached to the motorbike. He pulled something out of the bag, and when he whirled around he had a handgun pointing directly at her.

"Oh, you've got to be kidding me," she said under her breath.

She wondered if he even knew how to use a weapon. When they were together, she had never seen him even hold anything more than a kitchen knife, so seeing him holding a gun now was a ridiculous sight.

"You have to follow me! Rain, please!" His voice remained firm but near begging. "We can help you! I can help you. It is my duty."

"Do you hear yourself? You don't own me! I don't have to go anywhere with you!"

They were at an impasse. Both had weapons pointed at one another and neither one of them gave any indication they would move. Rain was convinced the howl that now shot through the air sounded closer than the previous one.

"Dan," Rain tried again. "You have no idea what you've gotten yourself into here. If you stay here, you're gonna get hurt! Look, I'm fine. I'll be fine. I don't need your help."

The forest began to shake with a ferociousness, the wind louder than before, the natural world seemed agitated by this disturbance. The sun had disappeared, but it still emitted a glow from the horizon. Not yet the darkest part of night. As Rain's eyes narrowed in on the trees, she clearly saw a streak of blonde fur amid the green.

"I will not accept no for an answer, Rain!" Dan waved the gun around with the inexperience of a novice.

"Well, that's the only answer I got for you."

Rain guessed he must have thought he looked threatening pointing a gun at her, but this silly display of power didn't scare her. She couldn't help but think that he probably had no idea how to keep her safe.

So Rain didn't know what to do. It seemed Dan's stubbornness would keep them from resolving things now just like Rain's stubbornness to save a doomed marriage had prevented her from leaving him for too long.

Because Dan had his back to the woods, he didn't see the wolf appear behind him. Animal footpads approached so softly, almost inaudible, further masked by the sounds of the wind.

Henry. The color of his fur had been burned into her memory ever since the day she'd seen him change right before her eyes. Plus, she'd never seen his equal.

Raising his lips into a snarl, the wolf followed with a growl loud enough to get Dan's attention. Dan spun around and started to shake at the immense size of the creature now in front of him.

"No," Dan breathed.

He raised the gun, unsteady in his hand, in Henry's direction. Rain froze, still with the shotgun pointed in the general area of the man and the animal but not knowing which one of them to aim at. Her breath caught in her throat as she watched the scene in front of her.

Even though she couldn't be so sure of the exact timeframe in which what she saw actually happen come to pass, it seemed to occur both in an instant and over a long period of time. Regardless, what she saw was unmistakable.

First, Dan fired his weapon, and the shot hit Henry in the shoulder. Yelping, the animal flew backward by the impact. Stillness. Dan then approached the downed beast.

"Dan, wait—" No more words had time to leave Rain's lips.

Only stunned for a moment, Henry sprung up with a thundering growl. She watched, her eyes like saucers, as his body expelled the bullet and the wound began to close.

Dan hadn't used silver, and a regular bullet had no effect on the creature, other than to piss him off. Dan began to inch backward as if moving in slow-motion.

The wolf leapt up, soaring through the sky at incredible height. His front paws landed on Dan pushing him down to the ground. Teeth glowed in the moonlight as one of his massive claws slashed downward through Dan's face and chest. Dan didn't even have time to breathe let alone cry out before Henry's glistening teeth ripped into his throat. When the animal popped his head up, it looked as if he'd dipped his muzzle in a vat of blood, dripping shining red as he pointed his head skyward and let out a resounding howl.

Next, his head darted toward Rain, standing on the porch. He took a step toward her. Rain's breath caught in her throat. She could see something in his eyes she couldn't discern. Malice? Hatred? Violence?

The wolf lifted a paw to take another step. But upon identifying the shotgun, which Rain still pointed at him, Henry stopped moving. A pleading look covered her face as she shook her head at him, feeling the tears behind her eyes threaten to spill at any moment.

In his eyes she then thought she could see something that, in humans, could only be considered recognition. Instead of moving toward her, he whipped his head around and with his enormous teeth grabbed what remained of Dan's mangled body and dragged it to the edge of the woods before completely vanishing with it into the forest.

Rain let all the air out of her lungs, and trembling, went back into the cabin and shut and bolted the door. Once inside she slumped against the front door and slid to the floor.

She took big gasping breaths like a fish out of water, and her eyes filled with tears. She couldn't say whether the tears were due to sadness or to terror. Either way, they wouldn't stop flowing.

It was the first time she'd ever seen Henry exhibit any sort of violence. But had he reacted that way because he felt threatened or was he trying to protect Rain? Animals primarily operated on instinct, so Henry's instincts must have told him to protect himself when threatened or attacked. She still didn't know how much human lived in the animal and vice versa.

She couldn't stop shaking but couldn't let go of the shotgun either, her breathing jagged and pained. She'd never seen anyone slaughtered like this before her very eyes. An eternity passed before the tears dried and her breathing steadied.

When she felt like she could cry no more, a pounding headache crept into her skull. What a time to be in a world without painkillers. Not too long after the dissolution of everything, drugs hadn't been too hard to find. But these days, medicine was a precious commodity, its prior existence a mere whisper.

Even though she'd been through every cabinet and drawer in this cabin, she decided to riffle through them once more to see if she could find any sort of headache medicine. A quick search left her empty-handed.

She was glad the supply of alcohol had been exhausted, as it would probably make her headache worse. She also didn't want to be too out of her senses in case Henry came back. One more wolf night left.

The thought of even trying to sleep brought on tremors, which shook her whole body, and she wouldn't even lie down without the shotgun by her side. She rattled the window and door locks, double-checking every last one before crawling into the bed and hiding under the enormous blanket.

The stress of the day had left Rain exhausted beyond belief, and though fast asleep as soon as she hit the pillow, she slept horribly. Her dreams morphed into nightmares, plagued by visions of violence and blood. She woke up more than once, her clothing and the sheets drenched.

One of those times of consciousness found her in the kitchen trying to pour out a glass of water, but her hands shook, spilling half of it on the kitchen counter. As she mopped up the spilled water with a towel, her eyes brimmed with tears that came out in big drops that mixed with the puddle on the counter.

Now she couldn't even lift the glass to her lips and spaced out staring at it before giving up and crawling back into bed. She dared not look outside. Even though she didn't know if Henry was out there or not, she was too afraid to find out.

Back in bed, she laid staring at the ceiling. She had no desire to sleep, afraid of what she'd see when she shut her eyes. Nor did she want to be awake either, existing in one of the rare moments where real life frightened her as much as nightmares.

The night dragged on. Outside, a quiet settled around the cabin. The wind was only a faint whisper now, and the only sounds were the gentle swaying of grasses or the occasional chirps from crickets. Eventually, her eyes grew heavy, and she gave in to sleep once again.

In the morning after the fog had cleared, she went out to where Henry had shredded Dan's body. The ground, dyed ruby, gave way to depressed grasses, clear evidence of a struggle. Crimson mixed with the dirt made a damp sienna color. Fresh tears pooled in her eyes as she shuddered at the sight in front of her, the only thing that remained of a life lost.

The motorbike now lay on its side, sunlight glinting off the chrome. She left everything exactly as it was and went back into the cabin, checking twice that she'd bolted the door behind her.

Rain made herself a cup of tea with shaky hands, and she sipped it slowly after curling under the blanket on the sofa. Over the fire she toasted a piece of bread and tried her best to nibble on it.

Her stomach twisted into knots. She felt hungry but sick. Fearful but worried. Her brain couldn't decide on one way to feel, which didn't help the situation.

After not making much progress on the toast, Rain tossed it aside and tried to focus sipping tea instead. A thought hit her like a slap to the face. Dan's people. She was certain at least one other person one knew about this place. If they were to come looking for him and discovered the bike here, it might be dangerous for Henry and Rain. Strange because Henry would be the last person she'd have to worry about getting hurt after the carnage she'd witnessed last night.

Her mind was a mess as she wrestled with what to do with the bike. She couldn't leave it in front of the cabin near the blood-soaked ground, providing clear evidence for anyone who came upon the cabin that something horrible had happened to Dan.

Could she even ride a motorbike? She had driven a motor scooter before, had ridden on a motorcycle, but had never driven a motorbike before. None of that mattered now because she decided she *had* to get rid of it.

She went back outside after packing a backpack. The keys were still in the bike as she hoisted it back to a standing position. She tried to recall her father taking her for rides on his motorcycle and remembered him telling her the left side controls the gears and the right side controls acceleration and braking. Sitting on the bike, she tried to get a feel for the clutch, ready for a lot of jerking around as she familiarized herself with shifting gears.

After sitting on the bike for a moment, tears fresh in her eyes, she practiced walking it to work on balance a little bit. Then she used the clearing to practice riding in a straight line, letting out the clutch, and then slowly rolling the throttle back to pick up speed little by little. It took her some time to stop riding so wobbly.

When she felt she could ride a little straighter, she practiced shifting gears. This took a bit more skill and more time than she thought it would. She wished her father had taught her, at the very least, how to ride a motorcycle. She did some trial turning around in the clearing, and after that she felt pretty confident about riding the bike into town.

This whole process took the better part of the day, and since she had to hike back, she worried she might get caught in the dark, never the safest place to be during a full moon. Worse than that, the clouds in the distance, coupled with the bitter chill in the air, threatened snow.

Troubled, she would definitely take the shotgun and packed some extra silver shells just in case. Most of the backpack she left empty, so she could fill it with anything she could find in town.

Over time the small town nearby had been seriously picked over, and most of their provisions came from the many abandoned houses dotting the surrounding area and beyond. She didn't have much hope, but she wanted to be ready just in case.

Rain rode the bike, not without difficulty or without a couple of minor falls, which sent tears streaming down her cheeks. But each time, she got up and got back on the bike.

The nearest town had to have been more than two or three miles away. She'd never been sure of the exact distance, as she and Henry had only been there on foot.

She remembered Henry saying he didn't like to drive, a funny thing to think of now. He knew how to drive of course. He simply had expressed he didn't like to do it, so anything they'd done together in terms of scavenging had always been done on foot.

Once she found out he was a wolf, she understood that he didn't need to drive. Four strong legs proved more effective at covering great distances, and he'd said he didn't mind walking as a human whenever he needed to go somewhere.

When she got to the town with its one strip of shops along the main road and several houses scattered on the outskirts and up the mountains, the afternoon sun blazed overhead. She parked the bike in front of a supermarket.

Next to the supermarket was a small shop, which looked like a jeweler. The windows had been smashed in and boarded up. Remnants of ripped down boards were scattered about, the place empty of any gems and jewels.

She laughed, peering in there. "So much for attempting to feel pretty today or any other day really."

In truth, she never cared much for jewelry, but had there been any, gems might have been a good commodity for trade. She guessed others had probably thought the same.

The supermarket's front windows had also been shattered, and she walked in, crunching a carpet of broken glass beneath her shoes. As she had thought, the shelves were empty, covered with the dust, garbage and debris of the past couple years. She continued on deeper into the supermarket heading for the storeroom.

An eerie quiet permeated the supermarket, the only sound the glass beneath her boots. When she got to the storeroom, she pushed the tall swinging door inward. Inside, she found it also badly picked over.

Her eyes were momentarily drawn upward to the exposed beams protruding from the high ceiling. A little farther in, she noticed there were a couple of boxes on top of a large shelving unit nearly as tall as the ceiling itself.

Since she was alone, she didn't want to set her pack down as it contained her only weapon, so she decided to climb up the shelves with it on her back. This proved more difficult than she had originally thought, and she almost fell more than once.

Once she got to a shelf too high for even someone tall to reach, she took off the pack and set it close to the wall. One more shelf to get to where the boxes were. She crawled up to the last shelf and peered into one of the open boxes. The bottom of one box was coated with some sticky brown liquid which had long since dried. She tossed it off the shelf with a groan.

Looking into the other box, a small unopened bag of brown rice took her by surprise. She wanted to believe it had been left by some benevolent soul and not left because someone had been assaulted or murdered mid-scavenge. She grabbed the bag and climbed down to the shelf where she'd secured her pack, and then hopped the rest of the way down.

Stepping outside she saw the sun had moved farther toward the horizon. Rain wondered if she should bother checking out one of the nearby houses, another shop, or start walking back to the cabin.

Not wanting to race the clock, nor being a fast runner, made her skin prickle with worry at the thought of having to race the sun. In the end, she decided if she could be quick about it, she'd have time to check out one of the other shops near the supermarket.

It looked like it'd been a coffee shop. Inside, tables and chairs were overturned, the cash drawers stood open, and broken glass lay all over the floor. She ignored the front of the shop and ventured into the small back room, which was about the size of a closet, and barren.

She searched through trash, scattering dust which hung about shelves like a thick fog. Coffee beans littered every surface, some next to a coagulated pool that looked like it had been milk at some point.

A single tea bag and two sugar packets proved to be a better bounty than she'd hoped for. She hadn't expected to find anything at all but still wished she had more time.

When she got back outside, the sun had moved even more toward the horizon, though she thought she hadn't been searching *that* long. Shorter days and colder nights.

Rain zipped up her jacket and started walking back to the cabin, keeping her hands on the shotgun and eyes sharp on her surroundings at all times. She cut through the forest to save time not wanting to push her luck with the setting sun.

The sun had sunk below the mountains and snowflakes fluttered down from the clouds above just as she reached the porch steps. She hurried inside and bolted the door behind her, exhaling in relief.

25 Brown Rice

THE MIDDAY SUN shone on Rain as she tromped through a thick layer of snow out to the well. She stopped shaking from the chill long enough to draw a bucket of water from the well and haul it inside. She washed off her face and arms in the bathroom sink with the frigid water.

Passing out on the sofa last night, she'd stayed under the heavy blanket through the morning. Now exhausted and hungry, she thought she should try to eat something, but found herself gazing at almost empty pantry shelves. She put her hands on the rice that she'd brought back yesterday, hoping Henry would return with food.

Shivering, she tossed log after log into the fireplace building the fire to a roar. Then she grabbed the bag of rice and set a pot of water on one of the cooking racks. Being careful about the quantity proved ineffective as she spaced out and dumped the whole bag of rice into the water, several grains disappearing amid the logs.

Ordinarily, this minor problem wouldn't have been enough to put her on her knees in front of the fireplace. Yet, she watched the water boil with such a ferocity through a watery veil of tears. When she summoned the strength to pull herself off the floor, the rice had gone mushy.

Things were not okay. Of course, she didn't love Dan any longer. It had been so long since they'd separated, but she didn't want him to die. She didn't want anyone to die, let alone be ripped to shreds in front of her eyes.

As much as she tried she couldn't get the sight of that animal, the enormity of the wolf and the fountains of blood that burst forth from her ex-husband out of her head. She wanted to believe a bloodthirsty murderer didn't live deep within the bones of the man she loved.

With eyes still watery and red, she sat next to the fire, blanket draped across her legs, the over-cooked rice in a bowl in her hands. She didn't even lift her spoon.

Thoughts of Henry, the man, drifted through her head like clouds in the sky. She didn't want the animal taking up any more real estate in her brain. Even though they were the same "person," she tried to tell herself they were two separate entities. It had become the only way for her to cope with what Henry had done.

The man and the way his fingers delicately brushed her skin, the way his arms enfolded her as if protecting a treasure, making her feel safe, making her feel whole, couldn't be the same as the animal who'd taken a life in front of her. They were different. They *had* to be different.

After staring at a bowl of rice for far too long, Rain gave up and put it on the table with a gentle clunk. She poked at it several times with the spoon but didn't put any in her mouth. She loved food, cooking, and eating most of all but wondered if she'd ever find joy in these things again.

Contouring herself around a pillow, she hoped to be transported to the land of dreams as soon as she closed her eyes, but what a foolish thought. A curtain of blood appeared every time she tried to sleep. Rain finally gave up and worked on memorizing the ceiling and the skylight, finding patterns on the walls, and watching the night shadows dance across the room.

Finally, exhaustion dragged her into the depths of sleep. Her dream wasn't a dream at all but a terrifying nightmare where Henry and Siobhan traversed the lands bathing in the blood of innocents. After returning to human form, they were naked and wrapped around one another in a passionate embrace, screams of pleasure filling the air. Rain couldn't see the other wolf's human face, but her hair flowed down her back, long and black as night.

The moon began to wane, and at dawn on the next day, she found Henry naked and curled up at the foot of the stairs in the snow. His dewy skin shined, with only a small purple bruise on his shoulder where Dan had shot him. Rain stayed at the top of the steps, holding a towel outstretched to him. He only nodded and mumbled thanks.

He went out back and returned with a bucket of well-water before disappearing into the bathroom. Rain did not follow him there. She let out a small puff of relief as the door clicked closed behind him. It would take a little bit of time to build up the courage to tell him the truth him about Dan.

With hair shining wet and a towel around his waist, Henry emerged from the bathroom to find Rain sitting at the kitchen table. She felt him approach and her whole body became tense, fear persisting and anger starting to bubble.

"Hi." His casual manner burned into her as he took a seat.

"We need to talk."

"What do we need to talk about?" Despite his

cool exterior, he spoke with what sounded like concern.

Pressing her lips together, Rain sat with her thoughts for a moment. It hadn't been necessary to ever sugarcoat anything with Henry. He valued directness in his own speech, so she decided to employ that same manner here.

"The man you killed was my ex-husband. Why did you kill him?" Her voice was almost a whisper as her eyes went glassy.

Henry moved his chair closer to her, but she moved her chair back as if trying to get away from him. Reading her clear body language, he froze and looked her right in the eyes.

"*I* didn't kill him, the wolf did. But if you're looking for an explanation—"

Rain interrupted him by slamming her fist on the table, almost knocking over her glass of water there. "Yes! Yes, I'm looking for a fucking explanation!"

Henry tried to maintain an even tone, but his voice came out shaky at parts. "I don't have much control as a wolf. I can remember feelings, images. I remember fear at the stranger, your ex-husband. Fear for you."

"Okay, well, how do I know that the wolf isn't just gonna go around murdering everyone? Since you can't seem to control him."

"You'll have to trust me. I don't know for sure, but I do have a lot of experience with him.

Attacks usually don't happen without some sense of a threat or hunger, like most animals. The wolf doesn't hunt humans for food, so that leaves the rare times when he feels threatened."

Rain blew out a rough, jagged breath. "I love you, Henry. I want to trust you."

"I love you, too," he said. "And I never want to hurt you."

He opened his arms out to her as if to say "come here." After moments without moving, she crashed into him, tears spilling down her cheeks. He wound his arms around her tightly. She couldn't deny the feeling of security she felt with this man's arms around her. Rain thought if there were only times like these, where he held her like they were the only two people in the world, she could gladly live happily the rest of her life.

After Henry kissed the top of her head and her forehead, she moved her lips up to his. There was not even a hint of aggression in his kisses. They were soft like the fluttering of butterfly wings, each one laced with the breath of love. She cut the kisses short and pulled away from him, a frown forming on her face.

"There's more . . . " She had to be honest about everything now.

"Tell me."

"My ex, he . . . he wasn't alone. He spoke of other people, a group of people, and I think they know about this place. I ditched his bike in town, and the snow covered the blood out there, but . . . " Her words came quick, tumbling out in rattled breaths. "I'm afraid they'll come after you. And I don't want you to die."

Tears welled in her eyes. He responded by getting up and taking a step toward her, and when she didn't move away, he pulled her to him again in a hug that didn't feel too tight. "I'm not going to die. I can protect myself. And I can protect you. We can protect each other."

When he moved out of the embrace, his eyes were so focused on her that there might not have been anyone else in the world. Her breath caught in her throat, and she reached up and pulled his head toward hers. She kissed him then like the world was ending, and he matched her passion.

When she pulled away, he still had his arms around her, and she didn't want to let him go either. "I love you."

"I love you, too," he said. "So much."

When she thought back on her life, how many people had made her feel like she was the only girl on this planet? Not many, if any. But he had. The way he looked into her eyes, the way he watched her any time they did some mindless or mundane activity, the way she could always draw smiles and laughter out of him, and she, in turn, always grinned back up at him.

If Henry touched, kissed, and loved her always with that same passion, she could live a million years and never tire of him. She didn't need nor want anything else. People could live through centuries never experiencing a love like this. This was enough. Everything had been enough.

26 Fresh Goat Cheese

THE NEXT DAY Henry said he had surprise for Rain. He asked her to stay in bed for a moment while he disappeared through the bedroom door. He returned after a minute with something soft wrapped in brown paper and tied with twine.

"What's this?" She eyed the package with a hint of suspicion.

"Open it."

She ran her hands over the paper carefully before untying the string and unfolding the paper. She gasped. A perfect log of goat cheese, her favorite.

Her eyes sparkled. "Where did you get this?"

"I have my ways."

She raised an eyebrow at him, begging him to expound.

"I, uh, well to be honest, before I met you, I

found a secluded farm miles and miles from here. Actually, a wolf night brought me to it. I ended up killing and eating one of their goats. I felt guilty about that and vowed to repay them in some way. When I approached them as a human, they were more than happy to accept the offer of protection I made in exchange for the cheese, but I never told them I was the one who had killed one of their goats." Henry rubbed the back of his head.

"I don't think I can eat this!"

"I think you should," he said.

"Oh, H!" Rain jumped out of bed and threw her arms around him.

She wondered how he did that. He always knew the perfect gift to get her every time. He either had a knack for gift-giving, or he'd come to know Rain so well he knew exactly what would make her the happiest at any given moment.

She couldn't count how many times she'd thought of cheese, daydreamed about cheese, wished for cheese, easily her favorite food. She embraced him for a long time and kissed him over and over again. How could she ever repay this kindness? She didn't think she could even if she lived forever.

As he held his arms tight around her, Henry rocked Rain slightly. Preferring to sleep this way, they were still naked, and Rain's body tingled at the feeling of Henry's skin pressed against hers.

She would've been content to stay like this forever. But there was cheese to eat, so she pulled away, moving out of bed with a little reluctance. He followed her.

"So, I need your help." She tossed on a nearby black sweatshirt and pumpkin-print pajama pants.

"How can I help?" He asked, pulling on some gray sweatpants over his bare behind.

"I don't know if you're gonna agree to this though."

"Okay," he said with a giggle. "Now I'm afraid."

She laughed. "It's nothing bad. I just need you to help me eat this cheese."

Henry emitted a small laugh and then said, "I can do that. So like 50/50?"

"Well, 60/40?" Of course, she negotiated for more cheese on her end.

"What if we do 55/35?"

"That doesn't even equal 100!"

"I'm not very good at math," he said with an embarrassed laugh.

"Me neither, but I mean I was able to add that up at least."

"But there's cheese," he said, as if trying to distract her.

"Oh yes . . . the cheese."

So they shook on it, and Rain went right to looking through Henry's pack, where she found a box of crackers, a package of crispy thin breadsticks, a small box of red raisins, and a package of mixed nuts, almost like he'd planned a cheese board. Maybe he had.

Sadly, there were no grapes, but she cut an orange that they'd picked from the tree out back into wedges as a fruit accompaniment to their cheese board.

Opening the wax wrapping of cheese, she breathed in its sharp, pungent smell. Perfect. It wasn't a large log of cheese, but still big enough to somehow split 55/35. Rain unrolled the wax the rest of the way and placed it in the center of their wooden cutting board. She tried to arrange it in an artistic way with half of the package of crackers around it.

To the inside of the board she added the nuts and raisins, hard as tiny rocks, then decorated the edges with the orange wedges, and finally plopped the breadsticks upright in a tall, skinny glass. No way a perfect cheese board, but it made Rain happy nonetheless.

Henry looked at her creation with a hint of awe behind his eyes. "Do we need to negotiate for the rest of this now?"

"To be honest, I'm mostly interested in the cheese," she said.

"Well, I could be persuaded to part with another 10% for this orange."

"It's yours."

"Deal." He picked up a wedge of orange and sucked the flesh through his teeth.

They solidified this second agreement with an orangey handshake. After that Henry built a fire, and Rain carried the board to the table in front of the sofa, setting it there like it was a priceless artifact.

Rain gasped, remembering that the last time they'd been out looking for food, she'd found an old expensive bottle of icewine in someone's wine cellar. Henry had placed it on top of the shed, tucked under the snow gathered there. With the recent fresh snowfall, it had been buried underneath.

She was glad that she'd forgotten about it when tossing the cabin for alcohol. Reminding Henry of its existence, she asked him to retrieve it from atop the shed as she couldn't reach it.

At the time she'd found it, Henry mentioned never being much of a wine connoisseur himself. On the rare occasions he drank, he said he preferred more sweet cocktails. Rain knew even people who didn't much like the taste of alcohol would enjoy a nice icewine. She herself didn't know too much about wine but knew enough to know she preferred sweet to dry and white to red. For her sweeter equalled better, and older meant better for sweetness.

Perfectly chilled by nature's refrigerator, Henry uncorked the icewine and poured two glasses. He positioned one on each side of the cheese board, and they both sat around the low table in front of the fire, nuzzling close to each other.

Giddiness filled the air as they made every effort to touch, to kiss, and to even softly brush against one another. The mood lightened, and they could feel the air rich with love. Rain thought that if she didn't need to eat, she would be happy to spend the rest of her days with Henry's arms and hands always on her. But because she did need to eat, she was glad to be eating cheese.

Rain sipped her wine in between nibbles of cheese spread on crackers, which tasted somewhere between fresh and stale. Per their earlier negotiation, she watched Henry eat the remainder of the orange wedges with little noises of joy before tackling the breadsticks.

Warmth, food, and Henry. Two of those three deemed necessary for human survival, but the final thing Rain decided *she* needed to survive. She pressed her forehead into the curve of his neck and breathed him in. Today was, without a doubt, her favorite day yet. Perfection.

"There is something I wanted to talk to you about," Henry said.

His serious tone shattered the happy mood and Rain furrowed her brow. "What is it?"

"These people, that you mentioned, the ones

with your ex, I can stay here and fight them off if they come, but I think you should go."

"Henry . . . no." She breathed the words out, her voice quiet but quaking. "I'm not leaving you."

"I don't want to lose you." His eyes were dark and serious, as if losing her was something he couldn't even imagine.

"I don't wanna lose you either, but I'm not leaving you here to fight those assholes by yourself."

"Rain," he started.

She didn't let him finish, poking her finger softly into his chest. "You listen to me, Henry. I love you more than anything, more than I've ever loved anyone in my whole life. And you love me like no one has ever loved me. Even all the dumb, imperfect parts. If I walked away from that, it would make me the stupidest fucking person on the planet. And I'd like to think I'm pretty smart."

"You are smart." He wrapped his arm around her waist, moving her body closer to his.

She laughed. "I am! And I'm staying here . . . with you, man or wolf. I'm staying here, and we're gonna face who or whatever comes to this cabin. Together. Okay?"

His face hovered near hers. "Okay. I can see I'm not going to change your mind."

"Nope. I've made my decision. I'm staying with you." She pulled her bottom lip in with her teeth, and whispered, "I love you so fucking much."

"I love you, too." His lips moved toward hers, and he pushed his tongue inside her mouth.

She breathed a soft moan and pulled his shirt over his head, her kisses falling on his neck.

27 Mulled Wine & Christmas Cookies

ONE CRISP WINTER day Henry came back from scavenging with a plethora of "Christmas magic," as Rain called his finds. His bounty consisted of an old bottle of red wine, half a bag of rock-hard brown sugar, and a Christmas present for Rain. She couldn't see it entirely, but something stuck out of Henry's bag wrapped in his trademark brown paper tied with twine.

Before he unloaded the goodies in the kitchen, he asked her to sit down on the sofa, and said he'd be with her in a minute to give her a gift. She plopped onto the sofa a bit flabbergasted and also a bit ashamed since she hadn't gotten anything for him. He told her it didn't matter, and she didn't have to get him anything because he had just seen something she would love and picked it up for her.

While sitting on the sofa Rain bounced her knees, eyes darting around the room. Henry pulled the package from his bag, hiding it behind his back so she couldn't see it. He then joined her on the sofa. He took one of her hands, and turning it palm-up, pulled a large square from behind his back and placed it in her hand.

"What's this?" But she thought she recognized the familiar shape.

"Open it."

She ran her fingers around the edges of the present like she remembered something. Then she eagerly tore through the brown paper.

As she'd thought, she stared open-mouthed at a record, and not just any record but a Christmas album full of classic songs befitting the season. Rain's entire face lit up, and a wide smile, impossible for her to hide, spread across her lips.

"Oh, Henry! I love this! I love Christmas music."

"I know." He returned her smile, though smaller than hers. "I remember you telling me."

"Can I play it now?"

"Of course," he said.

He took the record from her and put it on the gramophone, wound it, and set it to play. Rain almost cried, and she embraced Henry hard. She held onto him for a long time and swayed with him to the music while so many happy memories of the times before flooded her mind.

Satisfied with letting him go, she decided to use the wine to make some mulled wine, perfect for Christmas. She poured it into a pot, which she set over the fire. It had been far too cold to use the firepit outside, and more often than not a thick mound of snow buried it.

She sliced some oranges, and those went into the pot along with some cinnamon sticks, cloves, and star anise. She almost laughed, recalling an old tin of cloves tucked away in her parents' pantry for the length of her childhood, having been there longer than they'd had any of these spices.

Neither one of them much liked the taste of red wine, so she heaped in all of the sugar Henry had brought back. Rain eyed the pot often to make sure it didn't boil, lest it cook away all the alcohol. A sweet and rich, woodsy smell crept into every corner of the cabin, as Henry flipped the hourglass to time the wine.

They settled into the sofa, Rain near the fire tending to the wine and Henry with his guitar. He strummed along with the song "It's Beginning to Look a Lot Like Christmas," and Rain couldn't think of a better song to capture the moment.

She wished they had a proper Christmas with a tree and presents, piles of Christmas cookies, and strings of twinkling lights. However, like most things that were substitutes for those in the previous world, what they had right now would have to suffice.

All the while, Rain watched the hourglass for an hour to pass, and when it did, she took the pot back into the kitchen and strained out the larger spices and the orange slices. After ladling the piping hot wine into two mugs, she immediately put her nose up to her own cup, breathing in the scent of Christmas in a mug. She handed the other to Henry, and they snuggled together under a blanket in front of the fire watching the snow which had begun to fall.

The fire was jumping, and soon they were warm both outside and in. In one hand, Rain gripped her mug, sipping the hot wine. With her other hand, starting at the crown of Henry's head, she pulled her fingers down through his hair while his hand rested on one of her thighs.

Her whole body relaxed, easing out the tension of recent events little by little. These past few months held the weight of a much longer period of time, and there hadn't been much leisure time.

When they finally got around to discussing it, neither one of them had any particular thoughts about how they'd spend the day. Rain asked Henry if he wanted to part with some of the newly replenished peanut butter stash to make no-bake cookies. She used to make these with butter, but wondered if she could substitute coconut oil because once cold, coconut oil solidified nicely. Not to mention they were lucky to have an entire outdoor refrigerator.

Of course, he agreed to relinquish a jar of peanut butter because he said it meant he got to eat it in cookie form. Because Henry had spent many early mornings braving the snow, their food supply had now been built up to one where they could not only survive the winter, they could also be a little freer with their supplies once in a while. What better time than Christmas?

She started by melting the coconut oil and then whisking in cocoa powder, what little white sugar they had left, and a some canned coconut milk. She dumped in oats and scooped in peanut butter and added a couple dashes of vanilla to finish it off.

Spoonfuls of the mixture went onto a cookie sheet, and Rain left the small rocky mountains to cool at room temperature. Yet she couldn't help sampling some of it herself, taking a spoonful into her mouth and then feeding one to Henry. He expressed approval at the use of his precious peanut butter, and it amazed Rain how delicious these were, considering how much she altered the recipe.

Fortunately, she remembered making these cookies way back when she first learned to cook, so now she could make them to help celebrate Christmas. Even if they didn't know the exact day, it was close enough. Everything worked out. Although they weren't expressly Christmas cookies, nor would they be ready to eat right away, in her mind they made it feel much more like Christmas.

After solidifying on the kitchen counter, she put them in a container and stuck them outside, so they would not only stay cold but also stay solid. Cookies like these didn't belong anywhere near the fire.

Rain thought about what she could do for Henry for Christmas. Sure, she'd made the cookies, but she didn't think they were a sufficient present and wanted to give him something else. She thought about clothes, maybe making him a shirt, but quickly threw that idea out the window, remembering she hated sewing for other people. Plus, she never thought of herself as an expert seamstress. A hobby should be fun, not work. Making clothes usually felt like work.

During the time they'd been together, she'd made him many delicious foods but couldn't think of one food in particular which would make a spectacular Christmas present.

She remembered the drawing she'd done of them kissing and wondered if would be worth polishing up, framing, and giving to Henry as a Christmas gift. She'd have to wait until Henry went to bed, so at the very least she could have a little surprise for him.

The day of listening to Christmas music, drinking mulled wine, dancing in front of the fire, and cuddling turned into a night of Henry reading to Rain in between more cuddling and plenty of kisses.

Soon Henry grew tired and wanted to sleep. He asked if Rain would join him, but since she had plans with the art, she declined in her sweetest voice, saying she wanted to stay up a little longer and read a book she'd been trying to finish.

He embraced her for a long time, covering her in kisses. This wonderful goodnight almost distracted her as she felt an ache to join him naked in bed. However, she pulled herself away from all his sexiness, so she could surprise him in the morning with a special Christmas present.

After watching Henry melt into the bed sheets, Rain went digging through the art. Luckily, Henry hadn't added any drawings to the sketchbook which meant he hadn't seen Rain's drawing. The animated style sketch of Henry passionately kissing Rain with his hair blown back off his shoulders by the wind needed some cleaning up, some evening out of some rough lines. So she spent some time doing that until she felt satisfied with it.

Then she went riffling through one of the

large kitchen drawers at the bottom of the kitchen island. She had remembered seeing some picture frames of various sizes when she'd first explored the kitchen.

At the time she had wondered if they ever had photos in them or if they were surplus photo frames stored for future use. However, now that she thought about it, she further thought maybe these frames had been filled with photos of whoever inhabited this cabin prior to Henry. Because she had the feeling he hadn't owned it to begin with, she made a mental note to ask him about it later.

In the drawer she found a small frame the perfect size for her drawing, and she figured she could reuse the paper Henry had wrapped her Christmas album in. Once she had the drawing cut flush to match the frame, framed and wrapped, she put the present somewhere she hoped Henry wouldn't find it.

Satisfied with everything for the night, she pulled off her baggy black sweatshirt and pajama pants and crawled into bed next to Henry. As if by instinct, his arms went around her, and he pulled her body snug next to his.

She exhaled full of relief to be finally bathing in his eternal warmth on this cold night. He always made it seem not like winter at all. She tangled her legs in his and wondered if she should wake him up because she suddenly kind of wanted him. In the end, however, she decided to let him sleep and with that thought closed her eyes, happy and warm.

28 Carrot Tomato Soup

IN THE MORNING Rain practically sparkled, eager to give Henry his Christmas present, but wringing her hands over and over, she worried whether he'd like it or not.

But first things first. Breakfast. Rain pulled out a can of pureed tomatoes and a can of cut carrots from the pantry. She drained and reserved most of the liquid from the carrots and then mashed them in a big bowl until they resembled baby food. This was the best she could do without electricity and a blender.

She put the smashed carrots and tomatoes into a pot with some water and the carrot liquid and placed it on the rack over the fire. The soup started to form tiny bubbles as she added dried parsley, some garlic and onion powder, salt and a splash of balsamic vinegar.

While the soup simmered, the remaining

cheese was about to become grilled cheese sandwiches using a freshly baked loaf of bread. The ultimate comfort food. Every time she walked into the pantry and didn't gaze on empty shelves, she felt so lucky that they'd been able to replenish their supply of food little by little.

Henry helped by making the grilled cheese sandwiches after he asked her more than once if she did, in fact, want to share the rest of the cheese with him. He said it was her gift after all and didn't need to share it with him. But she thought, what was good food if not to be shared with someone you love? And she loved Henry above everything else, even cheese.

Their smiles warmed the room. She couldn't believe anything in this world could be so delicious. The carrots acted as a natural sweetener toning down the acidity of the tomatoes in the absence of sugar. There were no words to describe the euphoria of eating a grilled cheese sandwich when one hadn't had such a meal in years.

Once they finished, Henry gave Rain an abundance of hugs, expressing his gratitude. While she always loved his hugs, her mind drifted to the Christmas present she had for him.

She got up and went fishing through the drawer where she'd hidden the gift but felt a rush of nerves, fidgeting with the wrapping as she carried it over. She approached Henry with a half smile.

"Please don't hate it." Rain shoved the package toward him with her head bowed.

Furrowing his brow, Henry moved his head back, wide-eyed. He said he hadn't expected anything from her. She thought that those were always the best kinds of gifts, weren't they? The unexpected ones.

He spent a good minute flipping the package around in his hands as if studying it. Not able to take the suspense any longer, she urged him to open it. He tore through the paper.

"This is really beautiful! How could I hate this?" A smile spread across his face.

"I don't know. It's a bit scary to share stuff I've created and makes me feel vulnerable . . . even if it is for you." She paused and then puffed up her chest proudly. "However, I will say that this is the best hair I've ever drawn in my whole life."

"I think the likenesses are spot on. You're really good at hair."

"I just have a good muse," she said, winking at him.

"I'm impressed with that hand too. Hands are hard."

She breathed relief through her nose. "Thank you. I'm so glad you like it. I couldn't think of what to get you for Christmas."

"I love it, but you didn't need to get me anything for Christmas."

"I know, but I love seeing you smile."

Henry hugged and kissed her hard then. A certain sense of happiness had finally settled into their lives, and Rain felt relieved for the peace that came with it most of all.

He put the drawing on the table near the fireplace, so he said could always see it, even on the darkest nights. Rain felt a swell of pride at that because even though she thought her art was pretty good, she'd never bragged about it back when there were even people to brag to. Perhaps she should have done more boasting about it back then.

Not wanting to plague him with the same songs over and over, Rain asked Henry if he wouldn't mind listening to the Christmas album again. But not much of anything annoyed Henry. He nodded an approval, and she put on the record, singing along with every song. He said he found it endearing, saying one of the many things he loved about Rain was her childlike glee at the world around her. She sang and danced around Henry as he cleaned up the dishes, smiling at her from time to time.

Once Rain had her fill of silliness for the day, they collapsed on the sofa and snuggled close, trying to decide what to do for the day. As per usual, neither had any ideas. What was there to do in a post-apocalyptic world in winter anyway? Besides reading, cooking, drawing, playing the guitar, fucking, and scavenging for food and supplies? She tried to think of other things and drew a blank. Thank goodness those things were entertaining at least.

Christmas always stood in her memory as a time to think about family and good things about the year, even if things hadn't always been ideal. Now Henry had become her family, and even though things weren't perfect, nor had the year been for that matter, she couldn't ask for a better family. But what family was perfect? Or without quirks? It so happened Henry's quirks were dangerous, but she had decided to love him, all of him, even the dangerous parts.

In the time she had known Henry, despite the ups and downs, she'd become a much happier person, grateful to have a family like Henry, even if it wasn't the one she once had envisioned for herself. She didn't regret any of the decisions that had brought her to this point in her life. Love settled into every crevice.

Henry said Rain made him happier than he had been in such a long time, but he mentioned she didn't have to do much to make him so happy. She had to be herself, and well, that was all Rain could be.

In truth, this past year had been the craziest of her life. She never thought she'd meet a wolfman or she'd fall in love with one. Accepting him, all of him, had been the hardest part of this whole year, but when she did, she finally felt she could be truly happy. For once in her life felt she deserved the happiness that surrounded her in every corner of this cabin and the happiness Henry had brought to her life.

After mulling it over for some time, Henry and Rain decided to sit around and talk. There must be stories they had that the other hadn't heard. It turned out they did, so they set out on a mission to tell those stories in front of a roaring fire. And that was exactly what they did.

Henry told Rain stories about his life before he met her, and Rain did the same. Some were funny. Some were sad. Regardless, during this time both of them had their hands on each other at some point.

As usual Rain liked listening to Henry talk, and he said he in turn liked listening to her. The more she thought about it, the more they seemed to match on so many things. She said she would be content to spend the rest of her days, however many she had left, in Henry's company, in Henry's arms. In return, he said he would be happy to hold her as long as she needed him to. They whispered a hope that it would be the rest of their days.

In between storytelling, there were kisses and endless touches. They lounged every which way they could on the sofa with Henry only getting up to add more wood to the fire. At one point Rain got up to make some hot cocoa, but she made sure to add a splash of whiskey to hers. Warmth flowed through every room of this little cabin.

The stories turned to reading which then turned to more kissing which turned to heavy petting. Suddenly they were clawing at each other's clothes, trying to get them off as fast as they could while walking into the bedroom.

She hadn't anticipated wanting Henry in this moment, but this reminded her of how the first time they were together things came on in such a sudden and powerful way. Freed from the obstruction of clothes, his lips traveled all over her body.

He never stopped telling her she was beautiful. She drank this up like fine wine. Even when she didn't feel beautiful herself, he always told her that. His ability to see her beauty when she couldn't made her heart feel so full. She'd never experienced this kind of love before.

Henry's hands moved to her hips, and he pulled her body tight into his. She felt a rush of the warmth of his flesh pressed against her, and she reacted by shimmying her body even closer to his.

His lips moved on hers with a soft passion, lingering on every kiss trying to make each moment last longer than the previous one. She stroked his hair with one hand and gently pressed into his hip with the other. He breathed he wanted to be with her, to be as close to her as two people could be, in the very depths of intimacy. She nodded.

"I love you," he whispered in her ear.

She smiled, a slow relaxed smile. "I love you, too, all of you."

He wrapped his arms around her tighter, as she moved her hands over his body.

29 Campfire Potatoes

THE SNOW HAD BEGUN to melt, the days had grown longer little by little, and the sunshine had grown warmer.

Henry and Rain had gone easy consuming the surplus harvested oranges now stored in the shed, which doubled as a refrigerator. Thus, they had a steady supply throughout the winter, and they were such a joy to have around.

One morning Rain made an orange loaf. The others she used to make fresh squeezed orange juice, which they enjoyed once in a while at breakfast.

While Rain had been toiling around in the kitchen thinking about trying to be creative with the remaining provisions they had and making new loaves of bread, Henry had gone out scavenging. She breathed a prayer he'd return with new ingredients for her to play around with.

He returned early in the afternoon, and Rain went to meet him on the porch. He approached carrying a strange-looking black metal device, shaped like a large bullet. She knew it wasn't a bullet, of course, but had never seen anything like it before.

"What is *that*?" she asked.

He set down the metal object with a soft clang. "This is a smoker."

She looked puzzled.

"I can use it to smoke meats, and soon you can use it for quail eggs," he said, by way of explanation.

"Nice!"

The disappearance of the snow meant quails would soon be laying eggs. They might also be lucky enough to find duck or goose eggs which would not only be excellent smoked but could also provide delicious breakfasts once again.

Rain also thought the appearance of eggs meant she could try to make pancakes. She made a mental note to remember to look for maple syrup next time they went out looking for food, as neither of them possessed the skill to harvest it themselves.

"Also, I saw some pheasants on my way back. I suspect they'll soon start laying too," Henry said. "And I'll speak to my farmer friend with the goats and see if he knows someone who has chickens."

"Oh, this is great! I can't wait till I can get back to working in the garden."

She put her arms around Henry's waist, pulling his body close to hers. Things had been peaceful. Full moons had come and gone with no incident. No injuries. No former pack members.

It seemed like when the snow came, a calm had settled in with it. She'd accepted all of Henry and knew she deserved all the pure love and happiness he gave her.

This happiness, coupled with hope for their future, seeped into every part of their day to day lives. After everything they'd been through, joy filled her heart upon reaching the summit and gazing warmly upon the valley of their future. Henry rubbed her back and kissed her head like he often did. Everything felt right. She'd never known a more perfect love.

She didn't speak for some time, wanting to relish this moment as long as she could.

"Are you hungry?"

"A little."

She'd almost expected his standard response, and it comforted her to know a certain level of routine existed in their lives. Her breathy sigh of relief exuded that contentment.

"I made an orange loaf," she said. "I only

added like the two packets of sugar we had left, so it's a bit tart, but I think it's okay."

"Can't wait." He took her hand in his, and they walked into the cabin.

He left the smoker outside on the porch, saying it could wait until he had time to move it to the back by the firepit. Once inside, she sliced off two pieces of orange loaf, one for him and one for her. He tried it, and when his face puckered, she laughed a little.

"You do know that sugar is getting harder to find," she said.

"I know," he said. "It's not bad, just sourer than I thought it'd be."

"I had an idea this morning." She passed a potato to him to clean.

"Tell me." He scrubbed the potato she gave him. "How about we make campfire potatoes?"

Because they'd been liberal with them, their supply of potatoes had remained steady throughout the winter, and although it looked like winter had bowed out for the year, they still had a few left.

It surprised both of them that they had never thought about making jacket potatoes before. Funny how baked potatoes often got forgotten, though they were so simple to prepare.

Oftentimes, they got tired of eating potatoes despite the many ways they could be prepared. She remembered the time Henry had found ketchup, and they'd made French fries. What a wonderful food day.

In the evening, Henry moved the smoker from the front to the back. He set it on the brick surrounding the firepit.

Rain asked him to build a roaring fire, but only on one side of the pit. On the other side they would pile the embers transferred from the blazing fire. Among these embers, they'd roast the potatoes since putting a potato directly over the fire, even in a foil coat, would result in a burned, inedible fossil.

Once cleaned, Rain stabbed the potatoes several times with a sharp knife while making horror movie sounds to entertain herself and then placed each one in foil. Before she sealed the foil packs, though, she drizzled each potato with oil.

Cooking oils still remained easy to find; however, Rain secretly wished for butter because a potato dripping with butter sounded so good right now. Butter really did make everything better. She hoped a drizzling of oil and a generous dusting of salt and herbs could solve that problem as she seasoned the potatoes.

With the potatoes in her hands, sealed in their twisted foil jackets, she found Henry had started a nice half-sized fire in the firepit.

Like she'd asked, he raked the smoldering embers into a pile adjacent to the fire itself. She smiled at him as she walked out and set the potatoes among the embers.

He collapsed on the sofa saying he felt a little tired, but she crawled into the space he had left for her next to him snuggling close.

"Hey, handsome."

"Hey." His long arm went around her shoulders like it belonged there.

She tossed her head back and looked up at the stars, twinkling among the blanket of black in the night sky. There were so many of them there. She knew there were no more stars than usual in the world, but the lack of light pollution made them much more visible.

Rain always had a particular fondness for stars. They made her aware that Earth, this cabin, she and Henry were all such small things in a rather significantly large solar system, in an immenser galaxy, and an even greater universe. When the hope that she'd live long enough to travel through the galaxies faded, she was content to be the brightest star in Henry's universe, the one he gazed at more often than any in the night sky. With this thought she pressed herself closer into Henry's embrace, and he responded with soft gentle touches.

"I love you." She bristled a little at the abruptness of the words as they escaped her mouth, shattering the air like the logs cracking.

"I love you, too," he said after some time. "Sorry, I let my mind wander."

"Is everything okay?"

"Everything is perfect," he said.

"But you seem distracted."

"Not distracted, relaxed. It's a testament to how at ease I feel around you."

He kissed the top of her head, and then leaned away from her for a moment to pull some more embers from the fire and place them atop the potatoes. That done, he settled back on the sofa, and secured his arm around her again. She let out a soft almost inaudible sigh.

She felt happy, happier than she had ever been in her life. Listening to his soft, even breaths, she could feel he was too.

Turbulent moments she could do without, but she needed these moments right here. The moments of calm, of peace, of love. They made her forget about all the hardships they had endured to get to this point. Of course, she would never entirely forget.

Henry would always be a wolf. Though the future would undoubtedly have some additional storms for them to weather, she'd decided to walk alongside him even when he was an animal.

Hope told her they could do anything together. As long as they were next to each other, they were unstoppable.

30 Crackers

HENRY CONTINUED to disappear during full moons as per usual, and Rain tried not to think of where he went. During the coldest day, she pictured him running across snow banks or tramping over flattened dead grasses after the snow melted.

However, the nights prior and now tonight, the final night of the full moon, Henry hadn't vanished as he'd always done before. Instead, whenever Rain looked out the window, she saw the large blonde wolf standing sentinel outside the cabin. She smiled from behind the locked window next to the locked door.

Unlike before, she now felt safe with this animal as her own personal bodyguard. She wondered if her love had tamed him somehow or if the man inside had garnered the ability to better control the beast. Either way she felt better this full moon than she had in the past.

Letting the curtain fall back into place, Rain thought maybe she should make herself some food. Her stomach started rumbling, and she couldn't remember how long it had been since she'd eaten something.

Besides being hungry, she felt okay. Henry sat in front of the cabin. Rain considered the wolf positioned like this out there as a milestone in their relationship. She couldn't help but think their lives were moving toward some kind of normalcy despite the obvious abnormalities. There remained a pleasant absence of distractions and pain.

On her way to the kitchen, her eye caught one of the photographs of Henry and her. She picked it up and smiled, putting it in the back pocket of her pants.

Rain made her way into the kitchen pantry where she heard a rustling in one of the packages of dried food. Upon closer inspection she saw a definite tail. A small mouse must have recently found its way into the pantry, as she saw no signs it had been here a while, no holes in anything nor droppings anywhere.

Before it devoured any more of their dwindling rations, she had to get it out of there. She left the mouse to continue eating and went to the bedroom to pull a pillowcase off one of the pillows. When she returned to the pantry, the mouse still sat gobbling in the package of crackers. She tiptoed close to it, and in one fluid motion trapped the mouse and its bounty in the pillowcase.

Rather than set the mouse out behind the cabin, she wondered if the wolf might be interested in a snack. She twisted the pillowcase so there was no possible gap in between her grip and the part holding the mouse. Rain walked to the front door and eyed the shotgun next to it. Even though she felt somewhat safe, she guessed she'd better take it just in case. She unlocked the front door first in slow, sharp movements.

Outside the animal perked up his ears, and took a couple steps toward the cabin. Rain opened the door and emerged with the bagged mouse in one hand and the shotgun in the other. She took a couple steps on the porch. Henry took one more step forward and then stopped, eyeing the shotgun.

She'd forgotten how large Henry was in wolf form, almost double the size of a standard wolf. Rain felt safe to proceed, however, and leaned the shotgun upright against the railing of the porch just before the first step. It was windier than she'd thought, and the cross breeze blew her hair away from her face. She crept to the edge of the porch.

"Hi," she whispered to the animal. "I thought you might like a snack."

Using cautious, precise movements, she took the first step down, and then the second, and finally the third. Moving slowly, careful not to act in any sudden, threatening, or unexpected way, she bent down and untwisted the pillowcase, releasing the mouse into Henry's line of sight.

The mouse sniffed the air and started to hop away, but Henry pounced on it, and the next sound was his immense jaw crushing the small rodent, killing it at once. He gulped down the tiny animal, and his tongue moved along his blood-stained teeth, wiping them clean.

She shuddered, but still sat down on the bottom step with calculated movements. Henry sat down on the grass in front of her and then right after that, laid down. Rain pulled the photograph out of her back pocket and showed it to the animal.

"I feel kind of silly," she said. "I mean, I know you can hear me, but can you understand me?"

Rain had positioned herself a considerable distance between her and the wolf. Neither of them moved. For Rain, that was comforting. She didn't want to push the boundaries of whatever familiarity had been established here.

"This is me, obviously, and this is you." She held the photo up to him, pointing to the half-smiling Henry in the picture.

Henry got up and sniffed at the air in the direction of the photograph. The wind stirred a little, and he shifted on his feet. She dropped her hand and stared at this beautiful creature, golden fur shimmering in the sunlight. She wondered if she could pet him, but she decided better of it and kept her hand down.

"I miss you and love you so freaking much," she whispered to the man inside the beast. "I always miss you when you're gone. But I'm kinda glad you're here tonight."

He inched closer to her, his tail high making him appear even larger than he actually was. Looking down at the photograph, Rain ran her fingers around the edges of it.

She closed her eyes and thought of Henry's long arms wrapped around her, their bodies pressed together. How warm he always made her feel. She felt a sudden and strong desire to hug the wolf to see if the creature bore a similar warmth like the one Henry always transferred to Rain. She walked her fingers down her leg. She felt compelled to move closer to him him, to be close enough to reach out and touch him.

The wind picked up speed, and the trees in the woods began to shake with a ferocity that didn't exist before. Rain rubbed her arms, overcome with an abrupt chill from the wind.

A rapid swirl of wind blew in through the porch, and it whipped through pushing over the shotgun from its standing position. As it hit the porch with a booming crash, the gun went off sending a silver-filled shell into the clearing. Rain grabbed her chest feeling her heart about to burst through.

"Shit," she breathed the word out, taking several gulping breaths following it.

She turned her back on the animal, whose fur bristled. She climbed one step to retrieve the weapon. The wolf's ears shot straight up and his eyes darted to the shotgun. She placed one hand on the support beam to brace herself while she leaned forward for it. The animal crouched back down onto his hind legs. She lifted the shotgun, barrel pointed away from her. The beast's lips curled back slightly, bearing his incisors, and a low growl started to bubble from deep inside the throat.

The next thing happened at a speed no one could have stopped. The enormous creature sprung onto her, the force knocking her off the steps, and she flew into the dirt at the bottom of the stairs.

Rain let go of the photograph in her hand, and it sailed down to the ground like a feather caught in the breeze. His protracted claws punctured her flesh as he stood on her chest, and he twisted his muzzle back and forth as he ripped through the side of her throat with his razor-sharp teeth.

Unable to speak, she tried to form words, but no sound came out, so she only thought that feeling Henry's love fill every crack in her heart had been worth it. In those last few seconds, she remembered his lips on hers, his arms keeping her warm, and their laughter and the smell of food filling the cabin. She moved her hand toward the wolf's muzzle, not quite able to reach it before her arm dropped back down to the ground.

She tried to breathe but could only gasp. Blood poured from her body as she choked and convulsed. Tears streamed from her eyes until the light behind them finally went out, and her breathing ceased.

Her body lay still and cold, and a crimson pool spread across the chilled ground until it reached the photograph which had settled in the soil near where the garden had started sprouting again. The flood of ruby began to soak through the edge of the picture where Henry and Rain's faces now looked up into the sky, stuck in time and frozen in eternal smiles.

Epilogue

N THE MORNING, dew dotted the grasses in the clearing where Henry awoke as a man, naked and dazed, a short distance from the cabin. It always happened this way when he came to after the full moon ended, but he had never let Rain see this.

Examining himself through sleepy eyes, he found his hands and body covered with dark, dried blood. With no explanation, he decided to investigate the immediate area as he did whenever something similar had happened in the past.

While they shared the same body, the memories the other made were oftentimes separate, and even worse, sometimes wolf memories appeared in Henry's head as blurry or incomplete pictures. More often than not it took him a while to sort through and decode significant wolf memories. Therefore, he found it much easier to survey his surroundings any time he woke up covered in blood or wounds. Upon doing so he found Rain's body, a gaping hole at her throat, her eyes vacant, and her flesh like ice.

Whispers of the word "no" repeated over and over again were the only sounds that escaped his lips. He picked up her limp body from the cold ground. It was one of the few moments when Henry cried, silent tears like small, thin rivers streaming down his cheeks, but his sobs were quiet, contained.

He had a vague recollection of what had happened last night. Mainly the animal told him he felt threatened, which Henry couldn't believe because he knew Rain would never hurt him, unless he had been trying to hurt her.

Trying to recall the moments leading to her death, only gave him cloudy, fuzzy pictures like an old TV begging for a signal. He couldn't piece anything together. Nothing made sense.

He carried her blood-soaked body into the house. Once inside the bedroom, he placed her on the bed with the utmost care and then put on some clothes. He made sure to nestle his blue handkerchief, with the pink and purple flowers, that Rain had made him in one of his pockets.

Kneeling beside Rain's body, Henry made no sounds, but his eyes were still watery, red with silent tears. He tried to stroke her hair, but so much dried blood had matted it, making it impossible.

Finally, he picked up her cold hand, wrapped his fingers around it, and held it for an eternity. He couldn't see much through the tears now but whispered his love for her on an endless loop.

When Henry summoned the courage to let go of her hand, he picked up the framed drawing she had given him for Christmas now sitting on the table beside the bed. He gripped the frame in his hand for a long time before smashing the front of it into the corner of the table. Tossing the remaining pieces of glass, he lifted the drawing out of the frame.

Floating weightless like a ghost, Henry moved through the house collecting the other photographs of them, scattered around the cabin and wedged in various books. A devastating thought crept into his head: Rain had never gotten to use the last of the film in the camera. The fact that she never would brought tears to his eyes again. He creased the drawing and tucked the photographs into the fold before putting it into his pocket.

He returned to her body and kissed her hand. Her face, devoid of life, didn't resemble the woman he had known, as it no longer glowed with the spirit of someone who tried to find joy in the mundane. More than once he said goodbye and that he loved her, while whispering over and over he was sorry, so very sorry. Out loud he professed he would never forgive himself as long as he lived, and he couldn't even begin to think of how he'd get over this.

At this moment he was certain of only one thing. He could never return to this cabin again. This had become *their* place, and every corner here had been colored with memories of the time he'd spent with her. When he thought of the future, he would never have been able to exist here without her. Seeing a mirage of her in front of the fire or curled up into the sofa every time he looked at those places would have been too painful, so he packed a bag.

He gave her one last look before going to the fireplace and snatching the matches from nearby. He struck a match, and it hissed to life with an orange flame. He leaned toward the window. The lit match kissed the bottom of the curtains in the bedroom before completely catching on fire. He walked around the room igniting the sheets surrounding Rain's body, and a growl bubbled into his throat as he kicked over a table which shattered when it hit the floor.

Continuing through the cabin using match after match, he lit anything and everything flammable: the curtains in the main room, the sofa, more tables and chairs he had picked up and shattered against walls.

Content with the raging blaze, he grabbed his

bag and the shotgun and exited the cabin, standing in front of it for a long time. Henry watched the fire climb out of the windows and up the exterior of the cabin, huge black tufts of smoke billowing into the air.

Burning her body was the most just thing he could have done lest she be picked apart by rabid animals. Not to mention it hurt him to look at her like that, so changed from the person she had been before. Her body mangled, the light sucked from her eyes, her face joyless.

That shell on the bed wasn't Rain, the woman he had loved. The woman whose face lit up whenever she looked at stars or ate something delicious, the woman who danced around the cabin with playful steps, the woman who loved to see him happy. He only hoped he had brought more happiness into her life, cut short as it was.

Henry stood for a long time, watching the tendrils of flame curl up into the sky. Hearing footsteps crunch through the leaves of the forest, he spun on his heels to see a wolf with dark black fur colored with a light spray of tawny and a muzzle marked with a hint of gray. Siobhan. She sat down on the edge of the forest, where it met the clearing, like she was waiting for him to come to her.

Making no movements, Henry instead heaved a great sigh. He turned his eyes back to the cabin, as more surges of smoke joined the flames. He remained immobile for some time, and when he took a couple steps back, Siobhan rose from her sitting position, a movement Henry recognized to mean she was ready to leave.

But Henry didn't follow her. Taking his handkerchief, he wiped his remaining tears and held his head high, giving the smoldering cabin a wide berth, as he moved away from it and away from the forest toward the mountains, where storm clouds promised rain.

As Henry walked away from the cabin, his hand fell on the pictures in his back pocket, and he picked up speed, each step with more purpose than the last.

Six-Can Soup

Bonus Chapter

IN POST-APOCALYPTIC times there was no shortage of abandoned houses, but it took Henry months of searching before he found one he deemed suitable. Along the way, he'd picked up several packages of seeds and to his surprise, a dog.

The dog looked like some kind of cattle dog with a motley of gray, black, and tan fur. The most interesting thing to Henry was the black patch around the dog's left eye.

"Fancy meeting you here." Henry took a step toward it. "How are you still okay?"

The dog shuffled away from him.

When Henry pulled out an expired beef stick he'd found in one of the many houses he'd searched along the way, the dog watched with extreme focus. Once he tore the wrapper, the potent smell of the snack found its way right into the dog's nose. Henry marveled at the long-expired food and its ability to still smell the same.

The dog wagged his tail and approached Henry, and Henry knelt down and held out the food for the dog, which disappeared in a single bite.

He named it Charlie Crews.

After that, finding a new place became a matter of determining the right one with a basement where he could keep Charlie during the full moon. Considering everything that had happened, he didn't trust himself, and last time he checked, wolves couldn't unlock doors.

So when he found the perfect house, he took Charlie with him to find a home improvement store. As far as places that were picked over went, home improvement stores were raided of any snacks and beverages. Building materials and anything that could be used a weapons were gone, but things like locks, just what Henry was looking for, still hung on the shelves.

He pulled a key to key door handle off a rack and showed it to Charlie. "This should work, right? We can't open this without opposable thumbs."

Charlie cocked his head in what Henry determined was approval.

Back at the house Henry was now calling his own, he removed the current handle on the basement door and then replaced it with the new one.

After that he sat on the sofa. Charlie jumped up to sit beside him, and Henry scratched his ears.

Henry took several deep breaths and then opened up his backpack. Inside was a black rectangular box. Charlie sniffed at the box.

Turning the box over in his hands, Henry listened to the contents swish around inside. For some time he did this, unable to open it.

Finally, Henry blew all the air out of his lungs then opened the box. He set it on the table in front of him, just staring at it for a while.

He opened the box. Inside were some notecards.

When he'd had enough of just staring at the cards, he reached in and pulled out the first one. It was a note.

Dear Henry,
I know that cooking isn't your specialty and definitely not one of your favorite things to do, but I thought I'd write down all the recipes we made together in case you ever want to tackle them on your own. You know, like surprising me with a meal. ;) I have the utmost faith that you could make all of these things.
I love you,
Rain

Henry's cheeks were wet when he finished reading, and he was gripping the card so tight it had started to wrinkle. When he realized what he was doing he smoothed it until it somewhat resembled the card he'd picked up.

The first card after the note was titled Six-Can Soup.

"I guess we need to go shopping," Henry said to Charlie.

It took two days for Henry to track down the ingredients, which consisted of cans of three types of beans, a can of tomatoes, a can of corn, and a can of green chilies. The recipe card simply said, "Dump all the canned ingredients into a pot and simmer until flavors come together. And don't forget the seasoning!"

As night fell, Henry sat outside under the stars with Charlie lying at his feet. The night air was chilly, but Henry wasn't. He was never cold, something Rain had said she always loved about him.

He thought the soup was good, but couldn't help but think that it would have tasted better had he made it with Rain.

The day Rain has asked him to find notecards made sense to him now.

She'd been curled up on the sofa reading when he came inside from chopping wood. Since Rain had done the chopping last time, Henry told her to relax, and he'd do it this time.

When he came back in, beads of sweat shimmered across his brow. "I think that's good enough for now."

"That was fast," she'd said.

"Well, I had someplace to be."

"Oh? Where's that?"

"Right here."

He darted toward her, and she tossed her book as she scrambled to get up.

"No! You're all sweaty!" She thrust a pillow out in front of her as a shield.

"I thought you liked the way I smell."

"I'm not in the mood for your pheromones, mister!" She teased.

"Okay, you stay here not smelling like me. I'm going to go pick up some stuff."

"Oh? Well then, I have a request," Rain said.

Henry gave a dramatic sweeping bow. "As you wish."

Rain raised an eyebrow. "Do you think you can find me some notecards? It doesn't matter what kind."

"A new art project?" Henry raised an eyebrow.

"I can't tell you all my secrets, H." A smile pulled at the corners of her lips.

"I'll try to be patient."

Now, Henry sat eyes toward the stars. Rain had been so stitched into everything he'd done for the past year, he wondered if he'd ever not think of her.

"I hope she keeps coming back to me." Henry stood and looked at the dog. "Come on, Charlie."

The dog's ears perked up, and he got up, following Henry back inside the house. He barely made it to the bedroom before collapsing onto the cloud-like bed.

It must have been later than he thought. Charlie hopped up on the bed, curled in on himself and was snoring right as Henry fell asleep.

The next morning Henry explored every room of his new house, thinking of ways to make it his own. He'd never been a man of many possessions and had even less now after the fire.

To get to this house, he'd hiked high into the mountains, so it didn't surprise him when he found it mostly untouched. A thick layer of dust covered almost every surface.

"This will not do at all," he said, one hand on his hip, his other running finger over a table.

Some old rags, which looked like they'd been used for cleaning, sat at the bottom of the hall closet. He grabbed those and went from room to room, opening every window.

The air in the mountains was crisp, but the bright sunshine warmed the rooms.

While dusting Henry came across some framed photos of an older man and a much younger woman. One had a gold plate which said "Roger & Mimi: Santa Fe 2005." He collected all of them and put them in a drawer. He didn't need the former occupants of this place watching his every move. They were obviously long gone, like most of the world.

Once the house was mostly dust free and he'd swept the floors, Henry and Charlie took a hike deep into the mountains. Unlike the cabin he'd spent time in with Rain, this house had no well. But mountains usually meant some kind of waterfall or spring. It was just a matter of finding it.

Even if Henry didn't have much of an appetite these days, he'd still need water. In fact, he was surprised he was even able to eat the soup yesterday. He thought that maybe the card from Rain lifted his spirits.

Aside from Henry, Charlie would need water, too. It made Henry wonder where Charlie had found water before. Now, Henry felt obligated to find a spring since Charlie had followed him dutifully. Even if, as penance, he didn't want to do a good job of taking care of himself, he owed it to Charlie.

The more Henry thought about Rain and what he'd done, the more he wondered if he could ever forgive himself or if he'd ever want to look into a mirror without smashing his fist into the glass.

He looked down at Charlie, who tilted his head up.

"You would have liked her," he said. "She loved cheese and cooking and taking pictures. She was creative and colorful and funny. She cared about animals, and wasn't shy about enjoying things in life. And her fashion sense was great."

Henry looked down to see wet spots on his shirt and wiped his cheeks with his palms.

They continued hiking until Henry heard the trickle of water flowing down the mountain. He followed it until the stream turned into a pool of water. As he weaved his way through some densely packed trees, the pool widened and soon Henry was staring up at a waterfall, the spray tingling his face.

"We did it. Charlie, we did it." Henry looked at his feet for the dog. "Charlie?"

Before Henry could say another word, Charlie had zoomed by him and dove into the water. A smile tugged at the corners of Henry's lips and he felt a twinge of happiness for the first time in months.

After he'd filled up several canteens with fresh water from the waterfall and coaxed Charlie out of the water, the two hiked back down the mountain and back to their new home.

That night, Henry fell asleep stroking Charlie's head, Rain's drawing and photographs on the bedside table.

The next morning, Henry and Charlie went out on a food run. He'd noticed some houses high on the mountaintop that looked difficult to access and hoped he'd find some things there.

After searching the first house, he came out of it with a can of beans and some dog treats. Several houses later, he still didn't have much to show for it.

He was about to give up when he eyed one last house almost at the top of the mountain. He looked at Charlie, who titled his head at him as if waiting for Henry to make a decision.

"Well, why not?"

When he left the house it was with some packages of dried pasta and rice, which he put into his backpack. But what he was most happy to find, what he clutched in his hands now, were packages of seeds.

Back at the house there was a spot in the backyard that received the perfect amount of sunshine throughout the day. It was here with a trowel in his hands that he began to dig.

Charlie stood, eyes fixed on Henry for a long time. The dog walked around, observing Henry from different angles. Finally, he stretched his front paws out like he was going to lie down, but to Henry's surprise, he started to dig a hole.

"Charlie! Good dog!" Henry said.

Matching Henry, Charlie dug a number of holes. After, Henry nestled the seeds in, made sure to give them plenty of water, and then covered them with dirt, watering again.

Once they finished the garden, Henry went back inside and started to carve into a piece of wood. That took the better part of the day, which slowly dripped into night and drove Henry to the comfort of the marshmallow-like bed.

In the morning, sun streaks streamed into the room, waking Henry up. He dug his knuckles into his eyes, yawned, and went into the kitchen where the sign he'd made the night before was sitting on the counter.

Taking it outside to the garden, he hammered a stake into the wood plank and then drove it into the ground.

Then he built a fire in the wood stove, boiled some water, and then sat outside on the patio drinking his morning tea.

When he finished, he went back into the house, but not without taking a last glance at the garden for the day.

The sign read *In Loving Memory of Rain*.

Can I ask a favor?

If you enjoyed *A Year of Rain,* would you mind taking a couple minutes to write a review on Amazon, Goodreads, or any other book review site? The length of the review isn't important. Even a star rating coupled with a one-sentence review would benefit me tremendously, but more than that, seeing your feelings about my book out there in the wide world would mean so much to me.

If you or someone you love is struggling with alcoholism, please call the AA helpline at 1-855-831-2384 or visit www.aa.org. This could be the first step in getting better. Please take care of yourself, my friends.

Acknowledgements

Not too long after the pandemic began, I started a new job. In addition to navigating the harsh reality we all now lived in, I also had to come to terms with trying to find my way around an unfamiliar company.

I have been blessed to meet some amazing humans in my lifetime, no wolves thank goodness, but among those people were those who encouraged me to take up serious writing again, something I hadn't done for a while. It is because of that encouragement, that love and support from my friends, that this story exists.

Rain's story became a way for me to cope with the struggles being thrown at me daily. Like her, I didn't want any trouble. I just wanted to cook delicious things for my friends, tend to my garden, take pictures, and read. However, life has a way of being turbulent even when you don't want it to. I am eternally grateful to Rain and Henry for letting me put their story onto paper.

There are so many people I need to say thank you to that I'm always afraid I'll miss someone.

First and foremost, I owe the deepest debt of

gratitude to my best friend and number one cheerleader, Adam Bell, wolf expert and comma master. You were the first person to ever read one of my books, and your support and love of my story is what spurned me forward. Without you this book never would have seen the light of day.

Special thanks to Jessica Abreu, Heathyr Angellone, and Melanie Demoe for giving this book a very early read. Also, thanks to Jincey Lumpkin who gave this book a much later read. Your honest feedback was invaluable.

Thank you to Lara Wynter for completely redesigning my cover, helping me get this book more on brand.

I'd also like to thank my editor, Gina Kammer, for assisting me in making the story you just read the best version that exists in the world.

Though it was ages ago, it's important for me to acknowledge my high school English teachers Paulette Foley and Michelle Holyoak for teaching me to love reading. And while we're on the subject of books, Brandon Royer: I appreciate you for always giving me books that I had a hard time putting down.

I am blessed to have an amazing and supportive family, and that means the world to me. To all the awesome people in my life who built me up, made me strong, and taught me I could do anything, all while supporting my dream in one way or another, you know who you are, and you rock!

Tremendous thanks to my Kickstarter superstars: Jessica Harvel, Anna L., Andy McAllister, NeonPixxius, Lissette Buckley, Qavee, Corinne Brucks, Alyssa Akers, Brianna Welch-Martin, Terry J. Bond, Wes Chamness, Francesco Tehrani, Heiko Koenig, Aurora Springer, Paul Smith, Jeffrey Thurman, Scott Casey, Marya Jones, Krystina Roupe, Haabb, Mattie, Ashley Jill Murphey, Marcos Ramirez, Andie Vargas, John Idlor, Heiko Koenig, Starcy, Heyley Ingram, LaShane Arnett, Scott P. 'Doc' Vaughn, Roxas, Christie Cheshire, Tish Thawer, Ying, Jeremy White, Wil, Geoff M., Megan Wilcox, Tina Ox, Rebecca Hill, Michael J. Sullivan, Ellen Pilcher, and Fleur. Your support helped me make a gorgeous book that I never could have believed was possible.

And finally thank you to those who read and continue to read my books. I wouldn't be here without you.

About the Author

Jay Ishino has been an educator for more than 20 years. When she completed her BA in Secondary Education/English, she initially started teaching American and Multicultural Literature in Gilbert, Arizona at the same school where she graduated. She mentored with her high school English teacher and credits two of her high school English teachers, Ms. Paulette Foley and Ms. Michelle Fleming, as the ones who instilled in her a great love of literature. After all this time, she still considers Shakespeare to be her favorite subject to teach.

After teaching in Arizona for ten years, she moved to Tokyo, Japan to teach at international school and later transferred to a private Japanese school. While there, she got her MA in TESOL.

She has taught literature and Shakespeare to Japanese, Korean, and Indian students as well as students from around the world, entirely in English, for the past ten years.

Jay's journey to becoming a published author has not been a short one. More than two decades ago, she studied writing in community college which made her want to be a serious writer.

In her early 20s, she submitted a myriad of short stories to magazines. After receiving rejection letters from publishers, she decided to focus on her teaching career. Picking up her writing career where she left off so many years ago wasn't easy, but she started writing again seriously in 2016.

Today you can usually find her reading something she saw on Bookstagram or BookTok, drinking tea out of a mug from one of the many in her collection, taking pictures of pretty things, but mostly just being lazy with her dog pack.